LOOK OUT FOR MORE

AMAZING

MONSTERS,

TOTAL HEROICS

AND A BIT OF
RUNNING AWAY IN

The Shark-Headed
Bear-Thing

The Swivel-Eyed
Ogre-Thing

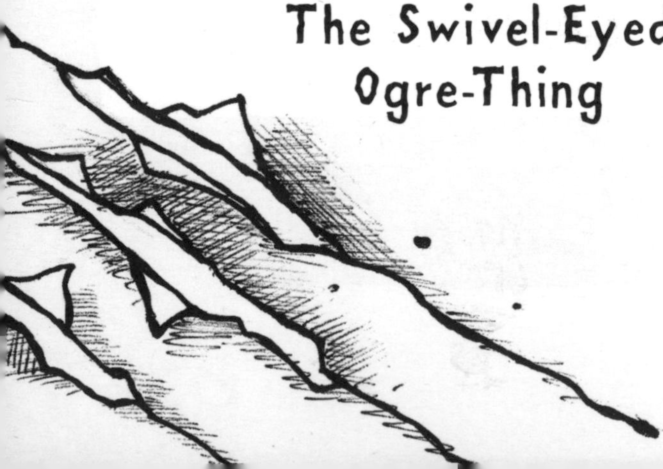

THE MOON-FACED GHOUL-THING

BARRY
HUTCHISON

illustrated by
CHRIS MOULD

nosy
crow

First published 2015 by Nosy Crow Ltd
The Crow's Nest, 10a Lant Street
London SE1 1QR
www.nosycrow.com

ISBN: 978 0 85763 523 5

A CIP catalogue record for this book is available from the British Library.

Printed and bound in the UK by Clays Ltd, St Ives Plc.

Papers used by Nosy Crow are made from wood grown in
sustainable forests.

1 3 5 7 9 8 6 4 2

FOR KYLE AND MIA,
the scariest ghoul-
things of them all

B. H.

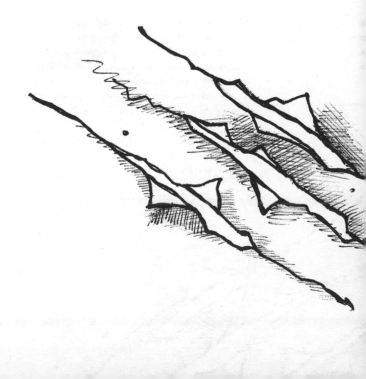

chapter One

Benjamin Blank stood in his bedroom
studying the little green-faced figure at the top
of his stairs. It stared back at him, tapping its
foot impatiently.

"Are you a gremlin?" Ben asked.

"No."

"A goblin?"

"No."

"Are you a big frog?"

"Of course I'm not a big frog!"

Ben ran a hand through his messy hair and
scratched his head. "Well, what are you then?"

Paradise Little drew herself up to her full
unimpressive height and pointed at the pointy
black hat on her head. "I'm obviously a witch."

"Oh," said Ben. He crinkled his nose. "Not
exactly original, is it?"

"Well, I'm very sorry," replied Paradise.
"I didn't realise we were being marked on
creativity." She looked Ben up and down.
"Anyway, what are you supposed to be?"

Before Ben could answer there was a
commotion from the spiral staircase that led
up from the room below. A brightly coloured

THE MOON-Faced GHOUL-Thing

head popped up through the hatch in the floor. Two large antennae flopped and flailed around madly on top of the head, like a couple of overweight worms having a fight.

Wesley Chant, former trainee wizard, climbed the last few steps. He only just managed to squeeze a pair of colourfully patterned wings through the hatch. "Ta-daa!" he said, when he finally finished clambering into the room.

Ben and Paradise both took a step back so they could take in the full majesty of Wesley's costume. He was wearing what looked to be a dark-blue body stocking that covered him from neck to toe. On his head was a red and yellow knitted bobble-hat with the jiggly antennae fastened to the top.

But it was the wings that really drew the eye. They were each over a metre wide, shaped like giant number 3s and sewn on to the back of the body stocking just below the shoulders. The detailed patterns on the wings perfectly matched each other, and Ben reckoned Wesley must have been secretly working on the costume for weeks. There was just one question.

"What is it?" Ben asked.

Wesley looked down at himself. "It's a butterfly."

"A butterfly?"

Wesley nodded. Quite proudly, Ben thought.

"Let me get this straight. It's the Feast of Scarrabus, the darkest night of the whole year, when children all over the kingdom dress up

THE MOON-FACED GHOUL-Thing

as the most horrifying
creatures their
imaginations
can conjure
up," Ben said.
"And you've
come . . . as a
butterfly."

Wesley blushed.
"You don't have
to dress up as
something scary."

"Of course
you do!" said
Ben.

"Yeah," agreed Paradise. "It's
pretty much the entire point."

"OK, yes, well, that may be. But . . . butterflies *are* scary. Imagine one kept doing *this*!" Wesley yelped, lunging at Paradise and waving his hands in her face. "Imagine that! Just doing *this* over and over again! Then what would you do? Hmm?"

"Kill it with a shoe," said Paradise flatly.

Wesley stopped lunging. His wings drooped. "Bit harsh."

Paradise turned back to Ben. "So what are you then?"

"All you've done is paint your face white," said Wes.

"I'm not finished," Ben said. "Turn round."

Wesley's wing slapped Paradise on the back of the head as they turned.

"Ow!"

THE MOON-Faced GHOUL-Thing

"Sorry!"

There was a soft rustling from behind them. It was followed a moment later by a *CRASH* as Ben fell over while pulling on a pair of trousers. He sprang back to his feet, fastened the trousers then snapped the hood of a cloak up over his head.

"Ready!"

Paradise and Wesley turned back to see Ben lurking in the shadows in the corner of his room. His white-painted face was barely visible beneath the black hood of a long robe.

Jutting out of the front of the cloak were two spindly tree branches. In the gloom they looked like long, insect-like arms.

"Well, I'm none the wiser," Paradise confessed.

Wesley's wings twitched with excitement. "Wait, I know this," he said. "It's the Moon-Faced Ghoul-Thing. Brilliant!"

"What's a Moon-Faced Ghoul-Thing when it's at home?" Paradise asked.

With some difficulty, Ben knelt down and reached under his bed. He pulled out a heavy hardback book and held it up for the others to see.

Paradise rolled her eyes.

THE MOON-Faced GHOUL-Thing

"Here we go again," she muttered.

"I found it in here," Ben said, flipping through the pages of *Who's Who, What's What and Why They Do Such Horrible Things to One Another*.

Wesley had given him the book soon after they'd first met. It was written by legendary monster-hunter Lunt Bingwood, who had mysteriously vanished shortly after he'd completed it. The book contained details of pretty much every monster and weird creature that had ever existed, along with helpful diagrams of the best places to kick them should the need ever arise.

Ben had had the book for just over six months and had read it from cover to cover more than a dozen times. He'd spent days combing through all the entries trying to find the perfect costume for the Feast of Scarrabus.

When he'd read about the Moon-Faced Ghoul-Thing he'd felt a flutter of excitement in his chest and knew he'd found the perfect outfit.

"Here it is," Ben announced.

He pointed to a creepy black-and-white drawing on one of the book's yellowing pages. The picture showed a tall, skinny creature with a round face and large bulging eyes. It wore a robe almost exactly like Ben's, but instead of tree branches it had six spider-like legs creeping out from within the cloak's dark folds.

"The Moon-Faced Ghoul-Thing," said Ben, his voice a low whisper. "Even Lunt Bingwood

THE MOON-Faced GHOUL-Thing

never saw one of these. According to legend it's the servant of Lord Scarrabus."

"I thought everyone knew this story," said Wesley. "When children don't respect the traditions of the Feast of Scarrabus, the Moon-Faced Ghoul-Thing snatches them away."

Paradise raised an eyebrow. "You mean like the tradition of dressing as something scary?"

Wesley glanced down at his butterfly costume. His face turned almost as white as Ben's. "I'm sure it wouldn't come for a silly thing like that. Would it?"

"Of course not, moths-for-brains," Paradise said. "The whole thing's a legend. It's just an excuse for people to get free sweets. There's no such thing as a Moon-Faced Whatchama-call-it."

From downstairs there came a series of soft chimes. Ben closed the book and slipped it back beneath his bed.

"Nine o'clock," he said, standing up and straightening his stick-arms. "You two ready?"

Paradise adjusted her pointy hat. "Let's get it over with."

Taking a steadying breath, Wesley smoothed down the wrinkles of his butterfly bodysuit. "Right then," he said, his voice coming out as a croaky whisper. "Let the Feast of Scarrabus begin."

chapter Two

The Moon-Faced Ghoul-Thing, the witch and
the bobble-hatted butterfly stepped out on
to the darkened main street of the village of
Lump. None of the lamps had been lit and it
was only thanks to the faint moonlight that
the children were able to see anything at all.

"Everyone got their bags?" Paradise asked.

Ben and Wesley held up two bulging cloth
sacks and gave them a shake. "Got them."

They strolled towards the closest house.
Shapes moved somewhere along the street
– other children out for Scarrabus's feast, no
doubt.

"I've worked out the best route so we can get

THE MOON-FACED GHOUL-THING

this done quickly," Paradise said. "The sooner we can get finished, the sooner we can all go home."

"Why the rush?" asked Ben, swinging his bag back and forth as he walked. "This is the first interesting thing to happen around here in months. The Feast of Scarrabus is supposed to be fun."

Wesley whimpered. "Fun?" he said. "Trudging around in the dark, surrounded by monsters?"

"Kids dressed as monsters," Ben pointed out.

"It's the same thing!" Wesley yelped. "I mean, no, obviously it isn't the same thing," he admitted. "But it's still pretty scary."

They reached the first house. It was one of the new wooden huts that had been built after the neighbouring village of Loosh had been destroyed. Loosh was supposed to have been rebuilt months ago, but a mysterious fire had burned every one of the houses to the ground before they could be finished, destroying the village for the second time that year. Not wanting to chance things a third time, the Mayor of Loosh had decided they should all just stay in Lump permanently.

Above the door of the house was a carved wooden fish. At least, it was supposed to be

THE MOON-Faced GHOUL-Thing

a fish, but the person who had carved it had either never seen a fish in their life, or had never had a go at carving before. Either way, it looked like a sort of melted slug with a very surprised expression on its face.

The hut was the home of pirate-turned-fishmonger Captain Swordbeard. From past experience, Paradise knew the captain had a fondness for kipper-flavoured fudge. She rummaged in her sack and pulled out a small parcel wrapped several times in thick brown paper. Despite the layers of wrapping, the whiff of sugary smoked fish was unmistakeable.

"I'm glad to get rid of this one," she said, dropping the package on the doorstep. She wiped her hands on her tatty black dress and all three children quickly backed away. Paradise began to march towards another house. "This way; keep up. You wouldn't want the ghoul-faced thingummy to come and get you."

She jabbed Wesley in the ribs. He let out a high-pitched squeak of fright. "It's got me, it's got me!"

Paradise and Ben both burst into fits of laughter.

"D-don't do that!" Wes yelped. "I almost soiled my body stocking."

Paradise slung her bag over her shoulder and hurried on ahead. "Come on, this is getting us nowhere," she said. "Last one to give out their sweets is a Gruzzleslug's mum."

THE MOON-Faced GHOUL-Thing

It took them almost forty minutes to stop by every house in the village. They left their little gifts of chocolate, fudge and other tasty stuff on every doorstep they stopped at. Some of the homes had already been visited by other children, and those steps were spilling over with stacks of sweet-smelling parcels.

Ben's stomach rumbled as he balanced his last bundle of goodies on top of a teetering pile of packages.

The aroma of toffee apples and home baking made his mouth water.

"We could probably take one or two," he said. "Nobody would notice."

"Are you *mad*?" Wesley spluttered. "And risk angering Lord Scarrabus?"

"Grow up, Wesley," said Paradise, rolling her eyes. "There is no Lord Scarrabus. If there was, why has nobody ever seen him?"

"Because we leave the sweets," Wesley said. His antennae bobbed about frantically on top of his head. "We leave the sweets and keep him at bay. That's the rule. Start messing with that and who knows what might happen?"

Paradise stooped and lifted a small paper bag from the pile. She fished inside it and pulled out a brightly coloured bonbon.

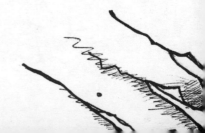

THE MOON-Faced GHOUL-Thing

"Are you seriously telling me you believe all this stuff?" she asked. "You honestly think that some all-powerful evil warlord is held at bay by children leaving chocolate on doorsteps?"

"Yes! Why else would the tradition have started in the first place?"

"Well, let's see," said Paradise. "Maybe because adults wanted a load of free sweets?"

"Ha!" laughed Wesley. "That's. . . That's. . ." He considered it for a second. "That does make a lot of sense, actually."

Ben eyed up the pile of packets. "So in other words, we should probably just help ourselves?"

Paradise shrugged. "Yeah, why not?" she said, tossing the bonbon towards her open mouth.

"N-no!" yelped Wesley. There was a brief flash and the sweet froze just millimetres from Paradise's lips. It hung there, floating in the air, quietly minding its own business.

All three children stared in silence at the sweet for what felt like a very long time. Ben

THE MOON-FACED GHOUL-Thing

eventually glanced sideways at Wes. "Did you do that?" he asked.

Wesley held up his hands and studied them front and back. He was technically a wizard, but every spell he'd ever attempted had either failed to work or gone spectacularly wrong. In the end he had been kicked out of wizard school after tests revealed he had less magical ability than the average door knob.

He hadn't been trying to do a spell, but he had nevertheless felt . . . something.

When Paradise had tossed the

bonbon towards her mouth he'd felt a tingle of energy tickle along his fingertips. It was like nothing Wesley had ever felt before, and – like wasps, sharp corners and certain colours of paint – it worried him.

Wes looked at the sweet. It was still hanging there like a tiny moon, defying the laws of gravity and common sense. Whatever the tests had found, Wesley reckoned there were very few door knobs that could have done something like that.

His jaw flapped open and closed. "I, uh . . . I just d-don't think we should eat them," he stammered. "Just in case the legend is true. We wouldn't want to come face to face with Lord Scarrabus, would we?"

Slowly, his hand trembling, he reached

THE MOON-Faced GHOUL-Thing

out and took hold of the bonbon. It vibrated
briefly between his fingers, then seemed to
relax. He placed it back in the bag, took the
bag from Paradise then set it down on the step.

Wesley smoothed down his bodysuit
and smiled shakily. "Right, that's enough
excitement for me. I think I'll call it a night.
See you both tomorrow."

"You OK?" Ben asked.

"Cock-a-doodle-dandy!" Wesley said, forcing
a smile. He winced. "Sorry, bit of a strange
thing to say. Don't know where that came
from. Um . . . bye."

He about-turned and took a few uncertain
steps along the almost perfectly dark street.

"Wrong way," said Paradise, who had a
special ability that let her find anything she

decided to look for. Not that she needed
magical powers to know where Wesley's house
was.

Wesley turned sharply left. Paradise shook
her head. "Still the wrong way," she said.
"Would you like me to walk you—"

"Yes, please!"

Paradise smiled and turned to Ben. She
punched him playfully on the arm. "See you
later, moon-thing."

"See you, tiny witch," Ben said. He gave Wes
a wave, then watched them walk away until
they'd disappeared into the darkness.

Ben waited until they were gone, then
looked down at the three bags of sweets they
had left on the doorstep. Wesley's words rang
in his ears: *We wouldn't want to come face to face*

with Lord Scarrabus, would we?

"Actually," Ben whispered, "who says I wouldn't?"

And with that, he set to work.

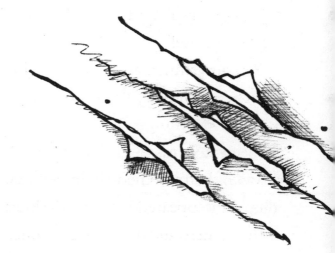

chapter Three

Ben stood in his bedroom looking at a large lump of rock. His uncle Tavish has moved it out of the basement and into Ben's room when Ben was out, to allow Tavish to fix up the basement wall.

Embedded in the rock was a sword. Only the handle and a few centimetres of blade

THE MOON-FACED GHOUL-Thing

stuck out from the stone. On the handle was
a detailed carving of a terrifying-looking
creature. Ben had searched every page of Lunt
Bingwood's *Who's Who, What's What and Why
They Do Such Horrible Things to One Another* to
try to find out what the creature was, but there
was no reference to it anywhere in the book.

Beside the stone was a long wooden box. It
was closed, but Ben knew that inside it was
the magic metal gauntlet that had saved his
life several times in the past. Both the gauntlet
and the sword in the stone had been found in
the wreckage of a wagon ten years ago. Ben
had been found in the same wreckage as a baby
and Tavish had taken him in, raising him like
he was his own son.

Those two objects were the most important

things in Ben's world. They were his only link to his past, and to the mystery of what had happened to his parents. As soon as Ben had first found out about the sword and the gauntlet, he knew he would guard them with his life.

It had been six months since he had last tried to pull the sword free, right before he and his friends had faced Dadsbutt the swivel-eyed ogre. Since then, life had been largely uneventful in Lump, and Ben hadn't thought about trying the sword again.

Until now.

Ben removed his cloak, used it to wipe off his face paint then hung it over the end of his bed. The cloth sack he'd used to carry his delivery of sweets was slung over his shoulder.

THE MOON-FACEd GHOUL-Thing

With the robe on, the bag had been completely hidden, so no one could see the sack was fuller now than when he'd left the house.

Pushing the heavy bag under his bed, Ben turned to the sword and reached for the handle. As it always did, a faint buzz of power trembled up his arm the moment his fingers made contact with the sword's hilt.

"This is my sword," he whispered. "This is my sword, and I am ready."

He pulled, then gasped. For the first time ever he felt movement, and for a glorious moment he thought the sword was finally going to pull free. Instead, the blade burrowed deeper into the stone, all the way up to the handle.

Confused, Ben pulled harder, but the sword remained fixed firmly in place. No matter how much he tugged, the blade wouldn't slide back out.

Ben's shoulders sagged. "Fine. See if I care," he whispered. He gave the boulder a kick, which he realised immediately was a bad idea. He jammed his hand in his mouth and hopped around the room for a few moments, trying not

THE MOON-Faced GHOUL-Thing

to yelp in pain.

Then, with a quick stop at the bathroom, Ben got into his two-sizes-too-big nightshirt, slid under his rough woollen blankets and lay on his back staring up at the thatched roof above his bed.

He thought about the sword. Why had it buried itself deeper into the rock? It had never done anything like that before.

He thought about the bag of treats stuffed under his bed but quickly began to feel guilty, so switched his attention to something else.

He tried to think about his parents, but he had no memory of them, so that wasn't easy. He spent a while rummaging around at the very back of his brain, in case that brought up any clues, but with no luck. The gauntlet

and the sword were the key. He was sure of it.
They'd help him discover the truth one day.

Slowly, gradually, Ben's eyelids began to get
heavy. He did his best to fight it, but after just
a few short minutes he drifted off to sleep.

Ben woke up. His candle had burned down
almost all the way, and now only a tiny flame
danced above a pool of liquid wax. From
elsewhere in the house he could hear the
rasping of Uncle Tavish's snoring.

There had been another sound too, Ben was
sure of it. Something had woken him
up. Something that—

BLOOP.

Ben sat up in bed.

BLOOP.

THE MOON-Faced GHOUL-Thing

There it was again. The sound seemed to be coming from the wooden trunk at the foot of the bed.

BLOOP.

Ben threw back the covers, crossed to the trunk and lifted the lid. Inside the trunk was a graveyard of old shoes, broken toys, interesting bits of wood and various other things he'd collected over the years.

BLOOP.

He dug around until he found a small rectangular metal box, then balanced it on the palm of his hand. After a moment, a small wooden bird popped out on a spring and said:

"*BLOOP*."

Uncle Tavish had invented the little gadget to detect magic. He'd named it the Automated Magic Detecting Device, because interesting names weren't really his strong point.

The bird popped back inside the box. Half a second later, it popped back out again.

"*BLOOP-BLOOP*."

Ben looked around. The bird was only supposed to pop out when there was something magical around. One *bloop* meant it had detected magic. Two *bloops* meant it had

THE MOON-Faced GHOUL-Thing

detected vast quantities of magic.

So what was it picking up on now? The sword had magical properties, and the gauntlet was a rare double-blooper. But they'd been up here all night; why had the device chosen now to—

"*BLOOP-BLOOP-BLOOP.*"

Ben jolted in shock. The Automated Magic Detecting Device had never given three *bloops* before. Ben had a vague memory of his uncle telling him that three *bloops* were very bad news indeed.

"*BLOOP-BLOOP-BLOOP-BLOOP-BLOOP!*"

The device began to vibrate violently. There was a faint *hiss* from Ben's hand as the metal suddenly became too hot to touch. He dropped it just as the spring went rigid and the frantic

*bloop*ing turned into one long *bloooooooooooop*.

There was a sudden knocking, like somebody rapping their knuckles on the door. The knocking wasn't coming from downstairs though. It was coming from inside his bedroom.

It was coming from the wooden box with the gauntlet inside.

There were no windows in Ben's room, but a chill draught made the hairs on the back of his neck stand on end. The candle's flame spluttered and flickered, plunging the room into darkness for a few moments.

THE MOON-Faced GHOUL-Thing

The sound from the Automated Magic
Detecting Device rose, becoming an ear-
splitting squeal that quickly became too
high-pitched for Ben to hear. He could feel
it though, like a drill at the base of his skull,
making his head ache.

The light returned, and Ben knew right
away that something in the room was different.
The knocking from the wooden chest grew
louder and more frantic, the box itself hopping
about in time with each violent *thud*.

There was the sound of rustling velvet
from above. Ben's eyes crept towards
the ceiling. The
knocking from
the box became
the splintering

of breaking wood as the gauntlet smashed its way free.

Ben tried to cry out but his throat had gone tight. There, half hidden in the shadows on the ceiling, was a white-faced figure in a flowing black robe.

Diving off the bed, Ben grabbed for the gauntlet. At the same time, the glove seemed to leap towards him. His fingers found the metal just as six huge spider-like legs snapped around him and dragged him, kicking and squirming, into the pitch-black folds of the Moon-Faced Ghoul-Thing's cloak.

The inside of the cloak was lit by a tornado of swirling purple sparks. Ben felt a prickling pass through him, as if every atom of his body were shooting off in different directions.

The cape
swished
shut. The
purple sparks
vanished.

And Ben was gone.

chapter Four

Ben fell, flapped his arms for a bit then thudded against a solid stone floor. He looked up and saw the Moon-Faced Ghoul-Thing clinging to the ceiling with its spider-like legs.

There came a short scream from within its cape, and the dark fabric billowed open. Ben rolled to the side just in time to avoid Wesley,

who hit the floor with a *crunch*, an "*oof*" and a
faint whimper.

A moment later Paradise fell from within
the cape and landed heavily on Wesley's back.
She sprang to her feet, jumping clear just as
three heavy bundles of material tumbled from
within the ghoul-thing's robe and thumped,
one at a time, on the back of Wesley's head.

"Ow," he said, then he rolled over, sat up
and blinked. "What happened? Where are we?
How did we get here?"

Ben pointed towards the ceiling, but the
Moon-Faced Ghoul-Thing was nowhere to be
seen. "Where did it go?" he said.

"Where did what go?" Wesley asked,
glancing nervously upwards.

"The Moon-Faced Ghoul-Thing."

Wesley let out a yelp. "It was here?"

Paradise unravelled one of the bundles of material. "This is my robe," she said, pulling it on over what looked to Ben like a big Babygro. Paradise spotted him looking at her. "It's a sleepsuit," she sniffed. "No jokes."

"How can you be so calm?" Wesley whimpered. "Aren't you worried the ghoul-thing might come and, I don't know, eat our faces off or something?"

Ben's eyed widened. "Well, I am now." He wrestled himself into his tunic, shorts and boots. "But we may as well be fully dressed and worried." He looked Wesley up and down. "Why are you still wearing your butterfly costume?"

Wesley wriggled uncomfortably. "The

fastener is stuck. It won't come off," he admitted.

Paradise took a wing in each hand, placed her foot in the middle of Wesley's back, then pushed and pulled at the same time. With a *rrrrrip*, the wings tore free of the body stocking.

"Well, that's one way of doing it, I suppose," Wesley muttered, slipping his bright-red wizard's robe over his head. Once dressed, he reached into one of his long, drooping sleeves and rummaged around until he found a pair of shoes.

"Don't suppose you've got a light in there, have you?" asked Paradise. The room they were in was dimly lit, making it difficult to see much of anything.

Wesley shook his head. "No. I haven't replaced the sun in a jar that Ben broke," he said, wriggling his feet into his shoes.

"We've got two choices," said Ben. "We can stay where we are. . ."

"What, and wait for the ghoul-thing to come back?" Wesley yelped. "Are you mad?"

"*Or* we can go and look for a way out."

"What, go into the dark and risk bumping into the ghoul-thing?" Wesley whimpered. "Are you mad?"

"Well, can anyone else think of a better idea?" Ben asked.

"I can," said a deep, booming voice that rolled like thunder towards them. Ben and Paradise both tensed. Wesley ran in circles, squeaked once then fell over.

THE MOON-Faced GHOUL-Thing

Two shutters rolled upwards at opposite ends of the room, letting light flood in through a pair of colourful stained-glass windows.

They were in a large room with stone walls and an impossibly high ceiling. Imposing bronze statues stood at every corner – statues of the man who currently watched them from his ornate throne.

At least, Ben assumed he was a man. Even sitting down, he was the biggest human Ben had ever seen. He could almost have given Dadsbutt the ogre a run for his money, and Ben wondered if he might be a miniature giant.

His skin was dark and wrinkled like old leather. The lower half of his face was covered by a black beard that was flecked with streaks of grey. It came to a point several centimetres below his chin, and looked sharp enough to have someone's eye out.

THE MOON-Faced GHOUL-Thing

He wore angry-looking golden armour that was all spikes and sharp corners. A headpiece rose up from the back of the metal suit, forming the shape of a snake-like mouth that looked to be swallowing his entire head. Deep-red jewels shone in the snake-helmet's eye sockets, and Ben would have sworn they were staring directly at him.

"Hello, children," the man said.

"Wh-who are you?" Ben asked, although he suspected he already knew the answer.

"My name," said the man, his lips drawn back into a dangerous-looking smile, "is Lord Scarrabus."

"Ha! See? I *told* you he

was real," cried Wesley, who'd leaped back to his feet. He chewed his lip. "Why am I saying that as if it's a good thing?"

"You're Lord Scarrabus?" asked Ben.

"I am."

"The actual Lord Scarrabus?"

"That is correct."

"The *real* actual Lord Scarrabus?"

Lord Scarrabus tutted impatiently. "Yes," he said through gritted teeth. "I am *the* Lord Scarrabus. The *actual* Lord Scarrabus. Anyone else who claims to be Lord Scarrabus is a liar because – and I really can't emphasise this enough – *I* am Lord Scarrabus."

The real, actual, accept-no-substitute Lord Scarrabus leaned forward in his throne and gazed at the children in turn. "And you three

THE MOON-Faced GHOUL-Thing

are in very serious trouble indeed."

Wesley let out a loud sob and blew his nose on his sleeve.

"You left no offering," Scarrabus told them. "You ignored the traditions. You disobeyed the rules of the feast."

"N-no we didn't," Wes yelped. "We left loads of offerings. We were at it for ages. You couldn't move for offerings round our way!"

"He's right," said Paradise. "We did. Something on every step, like the tradition says."

Ben didn't say anything.

"I thought you might say that," sneered Scarrabus. "They all say that. At first."

He sat back in the throne. To begin with, Ben had thought the chair was made out of old

driftwood bleached white by the sun. Now, though, he could see what it was actually made from.

Bones.

Lots and lots of bones.

Its high back had been fashioned from dozens of ribs that curved around Lord Scarrabus almost like a cocoon. The throne stood on four skeletal feet, and both its arms had bony hands with spindly fingers at the ends. It was either the greatest or most terrible thing Ben had ever seen, he couldn't quite decide.

"Where are we?" Paradise asked.

Scarrabus gestured towards a window on their right. It was tall and imposing, and featured a stained-glass image of a purple

dragon vomiting fire over a group of screaming villagers. Through the colourful panes it was just possible to make out a forest of dark, twisted trees.

"Goonderslarg," said Scarrabus.

Wesley's jaw dropped open and his eyes went wide. "The demon dimension?"

"No, a different Goonderslarg," said Scarrabus. He tutted again. "*Of course* the demon dimension. How many Goonderslargs do you think there are?"

Ben puffed out his cheeks. "Four?" he guessed.

"What do you mean, 'four'? Of course there aren't four. There's just one!" Scarrabus replied, his voicing rising until it was almost a roar. He thudded both fists against the arms of his throne, and Wesley let out a sob of panic.

Scarrabus clenched and unclenched his fingers, then *cricked* his neck. This seemed to cool his temper, and when he spoke again his voice was low and matter-of-fact. "My servant brought you here because you failed to lay your offering."

"But we didn't!" insisted Paradise.

"Oh," intoned Scarrabus, "but you did."

"Oh but *we didn't*!" cried Wesley. Ben and Paradise leaped back as a surge of energy

THE MOON-Faced GHOUL-Thing

crackled from
Wes's fingertips
and scorched the
carpet at his feet.

Scarrabus raised
an eyebrow. "A wizard.
Interesting," he muttered,
drumming his fingers on his
throne. The *tick-tick-tick* of his
fingernails on the bone echoed around
the hall. "Most interesting. Do you know
what happens to wizards in Goonderslarg?"

Wesley swallowed nervously. The energy
that had shot from his fingers had stopped as
quickly as it had started, and he had no idea
how to fire it up again. "Something nice?" he
said hopefully.

"That depends," said Scarrabus. "Would you consider having your magic drained from you drop by drop until you are nothing but a shrivelled lifeless husk as something nice?"

Wesley's throat was suddenly very dry. "Not particularly," he managed to say.

"And as for you two," he said, turning to Ben and Paradise. "I'm sure I can come up with something equally unpleasant."

Ben took a deep breath. He glanced back at his friends. "In that case, there's something I really need to say."

"And what might that be?" asked Scarrabus, raising an eyebrow.

"Run for it!"

chapter Five

Wesley and Paradise tumbled through a door
at the back of the room. Ben fell through
behind them and pulled the door tightly shut.

They had emerged into a hallway with two
sets of stairs – one leading up, the other down.
Ben raced for the steps leading down, but
Paradise caught his arm.

"What's wrong?" he asked.

Paradise wobbled unsteadily and shook her head. "It's. . . That's not down," she said.

Ben and Wesley both looked down the stairs. "Yes it is," Ben said.

"No, it looks that way, but. . ." Paradise glanced at the steps leading upwards. "That's down."

"She's gone mad," whimpered Wesley. "Leave her. It's what she'd want."

"No it isn't!"

Wesley hitched up his robes and set off down the stairs. "Don't listen to her. She doesn't know what she's saying!"

Beyond the door, Ben heard the thudding of footsteps. Grabbing Paradise, he charged down the stairs behind Wesley. "Up, down, doesn't matter. We just need to get out of here."

At the bottom of the steps, Wesley turned left and continued on down a second set. He immediately ran upwards past Paradise and Ben.

"Er . . . what are you doing?" Wesley asked, stopping beside them. "Why are you upside down?"

"We're not," said Ben. "You are."

Wesley gave a snort. "Don't be ridiculous. Why on earth would I be upside down? You're on the ceiling."

"We're on the stairs," Paradise insisted. "You're the one who's on the ceiling."

"I think I know the difference between being on the stairs and being on the ceiling," Wesley said. No sooner had the words left his mouth

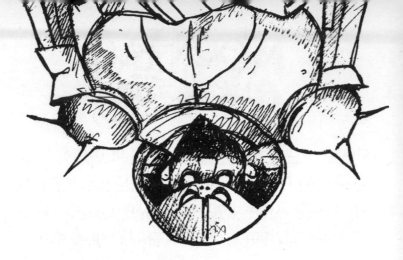

than his face went pale. "Unless. . . Oh no."

"*Oh no* what?" asked Ben.

"Goonderslarg," Wesley said. "Demon dimension. Different rules. Things don't work the same here. So up could be down, down could be up, sideways could be inside out, wrong way round, back to front. . ." He quivered with panic. "We might never find our way out of this castle!"

Paradise rolled up her sleeves. "Good job you've got me then," she said. "Like I told you, up here will take us down."

THE MOON-Faced GHOUL-Thing

She started downwards up the steps, but the rattling of the door handle made Ben catch her tunic and pull her back down upwards.

"Can't go that way," he yelped. "Follow Wesley, quick!"

He and Paradise took the steps two at a time until they caught up with Wesley. Sure enough, the spot where they had stood was now the ceiling. They looked up in time to see the wooden door open, revealing an upside-down Lord Scarrabus in the doorway.

"You can't escape, little ones," Scarrabus warned. "This castle is impossible for anyone but me to navigate. Run away and you'll be lost in the labyrinth forever."

Paradise flexed her fingers. "That sounds like a challenge," she said, then she set off down the stairs that led upwards towards the ground high below.

Ben and Wesley clattered after her. "Do you have any idea where you're going?"

"Half and half," she admitted. "It's hard to find my bearings. Everything keeps shifting around. See?"

She stopped abruptly. Ben and Wesley were only a few steps behind, but Paradise now appeared to be running straight up a wall. She stood there, sticking out from the brickwork

THE MOON-Faced GHOUL-Thing

like a nail.

"You're on the wall," Wesley said, in case nobody else had noticed.

"I'm not," Paradise said. "From my point of view I'm still on the floor. Try it."

Tentatively, Wesley closed his eyes and stepped forwards. When he opened them, he gave a little gasp. "Now Ben's on the wall," he said. His face went pale. "And so's Scarrabus. He's coming. Leg it!"

They raced onwards, upwards and side to side, following Paradise's lead through the twisty-turny innards of the castle. Scarrabus followed, never running, just stalking them relentlessly. He was in no rush. He would catch them sooner or later, and "later" would probably be much more fun.

Paradise darted into a side passage off a corridor. A split second later she emerged through another junction twenty or so metres up ahead.

With a frown, she stepped backwards and immediately appeared back round the first corner, right beside Ben and Wesley.

"OK, this is getting weirder," she said. "And harder. It's making less and less sense with

every step."

"It's pretty cool though," said Ben. "Check this out," he added, leaping into the mouth of the passageway. He landed back in the original corridor, but much further ahead. Unlike Paradise, though, when Ben emerged he was upside down and standing on the ceiling.

"It's shifting," Wesley fretted. "The rules of reality are jumbling up."

Ben jumped back around the corner and landed, right side up, beside them. "What does that mean?" he asked.

"It means we're in great danger," whispered Wesley. "It means the next step could merge us with the wall, or turn us inside out or . . . I don't know . . . fold us up so our bottoms are where our heads should be."

Paradise gasped. "I don't want a bum for a head."

"Too late!" Ben grinned. Paradise responded by flicking him on the ear.

A booming voice echoed along the corridor behind them. "Given up yet, little ones?" called Scarrabus. "You can't escape my castle. You can't escape *me*."

"We have to move," Paradise hissed.

"We daren't!" whimpered Wesley. "Think about the bum-heads, Paradise. Won't you *please* think about the bum-heads?"

"I can do it," Paradise insisted. "I can find the way out."

"But reality's moving!" Wesley reminded her.

"Then we'll just have to move faster," said

THE MOON-Faced GHOUL-Thing

Ben. He gave Paradise an encouraging nod.
"Go for it."

Paradise took some short, sharp breaths.
"Stay close," she told them. "This could get
messy."

"Agreed," said Wesley. "If we really are
going to do this then we need to stick very
close together so as not to— Wait, come
back!"

He dashed after Ben and Paradise and caught
up with them near the end of the corridor.
They turned the corner together and on
Paradise's orders dodged left, ducked low then
weaved right, avoiding a series of invisible
wrinkles in space.

"This way," she said, picking up speed and
racing towards where the corridor turned

off into an L-shape. "There's a way out right around here. I can sense it."

Ben and Wesley hurried to keep up as they sprinted along the final few metres of corridor.

"We're going to make it!" Ben cheered. "We're going to get out."

"Never doubted it for a minute," laughed Wesley as they took the corner side by side.

They stopped running and stumbled to a clumsy halt.

Wesley's shoulders sagged. "I knew we'd never make it. I said all along."

Ben looked to Paradise. "What's this?"

"I don't understand. This was the way." Paradise frowned. She raised a hand and pressed it against the wall blocking the path ahead of them. "This was the way out."

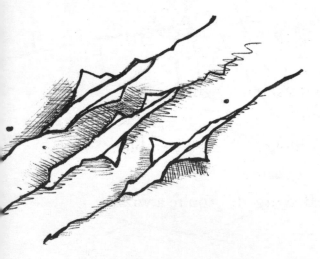

"Not any more," Ben said. He turned. "We have to go back."

Paradise caught his wrist. "Wait, don't," she whispered, pulling him into the shadows. From around the corner they heard the *clomp-clomp-clomp* of heavy footsteps – close, and getting closer with every step. Scarrabus was coming.

And there was nowhere left to run.

Chapter Six

"What do we do? What do we do?" yelped Wesley.

Ben squared his shoulders and puffed up his chest. "We fight."

"Fight? That bloke?" Wesley trembled. "We wouldn't stand a chance!"

"Come on," Ben urged. "You're a wizard."

"Trainee wizard," said Paradise.

"*Ex*-trainee wizard," Wesley added. "I got kicked out, remember? I got kicked out – and I really can't stress this enough – *for not being any good at magic*!"

"You froze that sweet in mid-air," Ben reminded him.

"You're right," yelped Wesley. "I'll do that then, shall I? I'll stop the massive angry demon lord by waving some sweets in his massive angry face. That'll teach him to mess with us!"

Ben blinked. "Do you think that will work?"

"No!" cried Wesley. "I was being sarcastic."

"Guys. . ." said Paradise.

"All right," said Ben. "No need to get nasty."

"Uh, guys. . ."

Wesley sighed. "Sorry," he said. "I'm just

THE MOON-Faced GHOUL-Thing

nervous. The last time I was this scared I actually wet myself."

"Ew," said Ben. "How long ago was that?"

"About six and a half minutes."

"GUYS!" Paradise snapped. They both turned to see her scowling at them. "It's a secret door," she said. "There's a hidden button."

"Well, what are you waiting for? Press it!" Ben urged.

Paradise stretched up on her tiptoes and pointed towards a brick that was several centimetres beyond her reach. "It's that one," she said. She shot Ben a glare before he could laugh. "No height jokes. Just press it."

Ben smirked and made a big show of stretching up above her head. "Oh, it's so high

up," he said. "However am I going to reach?" He pushed the brick. "Oh no, wait a minute, it's dead easy! Only a pixie would have trouble reaching— OOF!" Paradise thumped him in the stomach. "I warned

you," she said, just as a section of the wall rumbled inwards, revealing a dimly lit room beyond.

They hurried inside. Paradise pointed to another brick inside the room and Ben gave it a press. The secret door swung closed again and Ben wedged a broken brick into a gap at the bottom.

"That should buy us some time," he said. He turned to look for another way out, and that was when he saw it.

That was when he saw the creature.

It had a wide dragony head on a long dragony neck. Its bulky dragony body curled into a snaking dragony tail, and on its dragony back were a pair of neatly folded dragony wings.

All things considered it was, Ben reckoned, a dragon.

The entry on dragons in Lunt Bingwood's *Who's Who, What's What and Why They Do Such Horrible Things to One Another* was one of the shortest in the whole book. It was only three words long and read: "Don't be silly."

This was because, as everyone knew, there was no such things as dragons. And yet, despite that, there was no avoiding the fact that the thing in the room with them was one.

"A dragon!" gasped Ben.

"A what?" frowned Wesley, spinning on the spot. "Dragon!" he yelped.

THE MOON-FACED GHOUL-Thing

He ran back and forth for a moment then cowered behind Ben.

The dragon was smaller than Ben had always imagined them to be. Its body was about the size of a large bull, with a neck that was roughly the same length again. Ben had expected it to be huge and terrifying, but instead it looked a bit sad.

"He's tied it up," Paradise said. "Scarrabus has tied the poor thing up."

"Oh, thank goodness!" cheered Wesley. He caught Paradise's angry stare. "Er, I mean, *boo*! That's horrible. Tying up a poor ruthless killing machine like that. How dare he?"

Ben took a careful step towards the dragon. It tried to raise its head, but a chain slung over its neck made it impossible. Instead it just watched Ben with its wide dark eyes and blinked its heavy eyelids.

Its scales were a reddish-pink, with flecks of yellow where the sunlight coming through the window reflected off them. It had wide, flared nostrils and a short spike on the end of its snout. A length of rope had been wound around its jaws, keeping them tightly shut.

"It doesn't look like a killing machine," Ben said. "It looks scared."

THE MOON-Faced GHOUL-Thing

"It's not the only one," said Wesley.

Slowly, carefully, Ben reached out a hand. The dragon hissed and Ben froze. All three children held their breath, waiting to see what the creature would do next. When it didn't seem to be doing much of anything, Ben gently placed his hand on its head.

The dragon didn't draw back or try to pull away. Its wide eyes just kept watching Ben and occasionally flicking across to Wesley and Paradise.

"I thought dragons would be bigger," said Paradise.

"I think . . . I think it's just a kid," said Ben. "Like us."

"Only with wings and teeth and the ability to breathe fire," Wesley reminded him. "It's

dangerous."

"It's a prisoner," said Paradise.

Ben looked at the chains and ropes holding the dragon in place. He looked at his friends. "Not for long," he said, then he went to work on the closest knot.

"What are you doing?" Wesley yelped. "You're not seriously letting that thing loose, are you? What if it eats us?"

"Well, then you'll be able to say 'I told you so'," said Ben.

"That's not exactly comforting!"

"Stop whining," said Paradise, grabbing hold of another knot and frantically tugging at it. "Are you going to help us or not?"

Wesley hopped anxiously from foot to foot. He glanced back at the door. There was no sign

THE MOON-Faced GHOUL-Thing

of Scarrabus yet but he was bound to arrive
soon. When he did, the rock Ben had wedged
in place wouldn't keep him at bay for long.

Wesley sighed. "Oh, give it here," he said,
nudging Ben out of the way. His nimble
fingers worked hurriedly at the knot keeping
the dragon's mouth shut. "I'll get this, you do
something with the chains."

With a few short tugs, Wesley untied the
knot and began to unwind the rope from
around the creature's snout. When he was
halfway done, it snapped open its jaws. Wesley
screamed as he caught a flash of a flame
flickering at the back of the dragon's cavernous
throat, and then—

SLURP!

A long green tongue licked him all the way

from chin to forehead, soaking him in dragon
slobber.

"Argh, stop, getoff, getoff!"

"Hey, Wes," Ben laughed. "I
think it likes you."

Wesley wiped the drool from his
face. "Disgusting," he grimaced. "Still, better
than being set on fire, I suppose. Just."

THE MOON-Faced GHOUL-Thing

He set to work on another knot. "And it's *she* not *it*." Paradise and Ben both looked at him. "The little horn on the end of the nose. Only females have those."

"How do you know that?" asked Ben. "That's not in Lunt Bingwood's book."

"There are other books, you know?" Wesley said. "We did dragon studies in our first year at Wizard School, and as I repeated first year more times than I'd care to admit, I got to know quite a bit about them."

He looked down at the creature on the slab and frowned. "Although, since the first thing you learn in dragon studies is that there are no such things as dragons, I'm starting to have doubts about how accurate the course materials were."

Before anyone could reply there was a low *pop* and a sound like a lot of people whispering in the next room. With a swirl of purple sparks, a black cape unfolded from thin air. A large round face with an eerie white glow appeared next, and two wide staring eyes fixed their gaze on the children.

"It's found us," gasped Ben as a pair of long, insect-like legs extended from within the billowing black cloak. "The Moon-Faced Ghoul-Thing has found us!"

chapter Seven

"What do we do? What do we do?" whimpered Wesley as the Moon-Faced Ghoul-Thing crept silently through the air towards them.

"Keep going," said Ben. "Get those ropes and chains off. I'll hold the ghoul-thing back for as long as I can."

"Marvellous," squeaked Wesley. "Well, that should buy us about four seconds."

"Shut up and keep untying," Paradise snapped. "Ben knows what he's doing."

Ben, in fact, didn't know what he was doing. He had no idea how to deal with a Moon-Faced Ghoul-Thing, and it was taking all his willpower not to just shut his eyes, put his fingers in his ears and hope it went away on its own.

THE MOON-FACED GHOUL-Thing

Instead, he stepped between it and his friends, and held up the gauntlet hand, palm facing the approaching creature.

"Stop right there," he commanded. To his amazement, the ghoul-thing stopped. It bobbed up and down in the middle of the room, its bulging eyes flicking from the gauntlet to Ben's face and back again.

"Er, right. Good," said Ben, who wasn't quite sure what he should do next. "Now . . . go away."

The Moon-Faced Ghoul-Thing didn't move.

"Please?" said Ben.

The Moon-Faced Ghoul-Thing still didn't move.

"Well, that showed it," said Paradise. There was a rattle as a chain fell to the floor, and she hurried over to the next one.

"It's not doing anything," Ben said. "It's just sort of floating there."

"Well, don't complain about it," said Wesley, using his teeth to pull free a particularly tight knot. "Would you rather it was biting our heads off?"

"That'd be tricky since it doesn't have a mouth," Ben pointed out. "Just a head, some bug arms and a . . ." His eyes went to the ghoul-thing's cape. A flurry of purple sparks

ignited within it. ". . . cloak. Oh no."

"Oh no what?" yelped Wesley. Ben raced
to his side and all three of them frantically
worked at the ropes and chains that held the
dragon in place.

"Scarrabus is coming," said Ben.

Paradise's eyes went to the door. "No he isn't.
He's not out there."

"Not that way," Ben said. He pointed to
the ghoul-thing just as an armour-clad foot
extended from within its cape and stomped
down on to the rough stone floor. "*That* way!"

"Ah, there you are," growled Scarrabus,
ducking through the portal and immediately
dwarfing everything in the room. "I told you
you wouldn't get far."

At the sight of Scarrabus, the dragon began

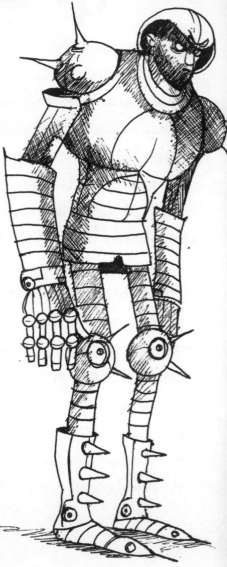

to buck and thrash
against its restraints.
The children jumped
back as the animal
squirmed and
struggled to get
free.

Scarrabus's face
darkened. "What
are you doing? Get
away from my pet."

"She's not your
pet, she's your
prisoner," said
Paradise. She barely
came up to Lord
Scarrabus's waist, but

THE MOON-Faced GHOUL-Thing

she stared up at him defiantly all the same.

"You are all my prisoners," Scarrabus pointed out. "Such is the price for failing to leave your offering."

"But we didn't," protested Wesley. He ducked to avoid a thrashing swipe of the dragon's tail. "We left the sweets; you've made a mistake!"

"It is you three who have made the mistake of daring to question the great and terrible Lord Scarrabus!" the demon-lord roared.

"And you shall all pay with your—"

A small fireball, no bigger than Ben's thumb, hit Scarrabus between the eyes. He looked up in time to see his eyebrows catch fire and spent a few frantic seconds squashing the flames out with his thumb.

The dragon yanked at the final chain holding her in place. The metal hooks attaching the chain to the stone slab tore free, and the dragon let out a bellow of triumph.

"Stay where you are," Scarrabus barked, but the dragon opened her mouth and shot three more tiny fireballs in his direction. He batted them away and raced to close the gap between them.

Ben, Paradise and Wesley were caught by surprise as the dragon weaved her long neck

THE MOON-Faced GHOUL-Thing

between their legs and hoisted them on to her back. They caught a final glimpse of Lord Scarrabus charging after them, then the next thing the children saw was the window. It seemed to be getting bigger.

"Hold on!" Ben warned. He and Paradise both ducked, leaving Wesley to watch in horror as the dragon hurtled towards the glass.

"Ooh," he grimaced. "This is going to hurt."

KERASH!

The window exploded outwards as the dragon and her passengers flew free of the castle.

"Woo-hoo!" hollered Ben, thrusting a fist into the air. "Best. Escape. Ever."

"We're flying!" gasped Paradise. "We're flying!"

The dragon's
wings flapped
frantically. The
world gave a sudden
lurch.

"Oh no. Spoke too
soon," Paradise said,
and all four of them
began to fall.

They tumbled
and flailed helplessly
through the air,
plunging down, down,
down towards the
distant ground below.

"The good news is
we're going to land in

THE MOON-Faced GHOUL-Thing

the moat," Ben shouted over the roaring of the wind and the screaming of the wizard.

"The bad news," he added, gesturing down at the glowing red river beneath them, "is that the moat is made of lava."

"Oh come on," Wesley cried. "Who has a lava moat? That's not fair."

"Do something!" Paradise shouted.

Wesley rummaged inside one of his robe's wide sleeves. "I've got it!" he cheered, then he pulled out a small umbrella and opened it. It immediately turned inside out, then fell to bits. "Well, that was disappointing."

Above them, the dragon was wildly beating its wings against the wind, but they were weak from being tied, and the flapping was doing nothing to slow the creature's fall.

"I meant magic!" hollered Paradise. "Magic us somewhere."

"I don't know how!"

"Try!" Ben cried.

"What if I send us somewhere dangerous?"

Without a word, Paradise pointed down at the rapidly approaching lava moat. The air around them was already becoming hot and thick with black smoke.

"F-fair point," Wesley stammered. He raised his hands and waggled his fingers uncertainly. "Um, sendus . . . elsewhereum. . . Pleeeease."

Unsurprisingly, nothing happened.

"Oh, it's no use! I have no idea what I should even be saying!"

No sooner were the words out of his mouth when Wesley's whole body stiffened. His

THE MOON-Faced GHOUL-Thing

arms swept upwards in an arc above his head, leaving a blueish-green trail shimmering in their wake.

He didn't speak. There was no need. With a flourish of his fingers, the world around them changed.

There was a *crash*, a *crunch* and a series of "*oofs*" and then, with three *thuds* and one final big *smash*, they hit the ground.

chapter Eight

Ben was woken by a stick poking him in the face. Groaning, he prised open his eyelids and looked up, only to see something short and skinny looking back down.

At first he thought it was Paradise in her green robe, but he quickly realised that this wasn't the case. The figure was a little shorter

THE MOON-Faced GHOUL-Thing

than Paradise for one thing, and it wasn't his
clothing that was green. It was his skin.

Ben nudged the walking stick away from his
face and sat up. This hurt. There were loads of
little scratches and cuts on his hand and legs.
From the way it ached to blink he guessed
there were a few on his face too.

His clothes were thick with grime and
broken twigs, and he was lying on something
lumpy and uncomfortable.

"Get off," said Paradise from beneath him.

Ben slid sideways as Paradise wriggled into a
sitting position and spotted the green-skinned
figure peering at them.

He was a strange-looking little man, with
a head shaped like a sagging rugby ball and
wide, bloodshot eyes that took up seventy per

cent of his face. There was barely room left over for his long pointy nose and his puckered little mouth that reminded Ben of an inside-out walnut. He had fluffy grey eyebrows, which wasn't particularly unusual, but they were on his cheeks, which was.

His clothing had been fashioned from a few old sacks, tied with a length of rope around his middle. He had stopped poking Ben with his knobbly walking stick, but the man now held it in front of him like a sword.

"Who are you?" Paradise asked.

"Who am I?" said the little man, his eyes darting nervously. "Good question. Good question. Here's another. Who are you? Hmm? And why did you fall through my roof?"

Ben and Paradise both looked up. Sure

enough, there was
a large hole in the
thatched roof above
their heads. Wesley
dangled upside down
from it, his robe
snagged on a piece of
broken wood.

"Hello there," Wesley said, then he fell in a heap to the floor. He bounded back to his feet and smoothed his crumpled robe with both hands. "I'm up, I'm fine. I'm fine. Meant that." He spotted the little green man. "Oh. A goblin."

"Where?" said the little man. "Oh, me. Yes. A goblin I am. Not just any goblin. No, sir. A Luck Goblin. Very rare."

"A Luck Goblin?" said Ben. He hadn't read about those in Lunt Bingwood's book either.

"What kind of Luck Goblin?" Wesley asked. "Bad luck or good luck?"

The goblin glanced around the ruined remains of his house, lingering for a moment on the small dragon that had crash-landed on what looked as if it had once been his kitchen table.

"Guess," he said and then, with a *ping*, his trousers fell down. He hurriedly pulled them back up. "Sorry, that happens occasionally. Well, regularly. Well . . . six times a day."

The dragon let out a happy-sounding little *yip* and wagged her tail as Paradise approached her. She looked like a big, weird-shaped dog. With wings.

"I think she's OK," Paradise said. The dragon licked her cheek, pasting slobber all over her face. "Yes, definitely fine," Paradise spluttered.

Ben looked at the damage around them. It had probably been quite a nice little house until a few minutes ago. The walls were made of mossy stone, and the furniture – what was left of it – looked quite rough and rustic, but it was pleasant in its own way.

"Mr Nuttendudge," said the goblin.

Ben and Wesley exchanged a glance. "I'm sorry?" said Wesley.

"Me. My name. Mr Nuttendudge," the goblin said. He held out a hand that looked much too large for the rest of him. Ben reached out with the gauntlet and shook the offered

hand. The goblin's eyes widened when it felt the metal against its skin, but he didn't say a word.

"I'm Ben." He tried to take his hand back but Mr Nuttendudge kept hold of it, his eyes firmly fixed on the gauntlet. With a firm tug, Ben pulled it free and gestured to the others. "This is Wesley; that's Paradise."

"Ben, Wesley, Paradise," said Mr Nuttendudge. He repeated their names a few times, then gave a nod. "And who is your young dragon friend?"

"She's, um. . ." Ben began. "Actually, we don't know what her name—"

"Burnie," announced Paradise. "Her name's Burnie."

Ben opened his mouth to argue but Paradise

shot him one of her looks. He shrugged. "Yeah, looks like we're going with that."

Mr Nuttendudge nodded. "Apt. Good. Appropriate. Not often you see a dragon. Especially not in my kitchen."

With some difficulty he pulled a small wooden chair free of the wreckage, dusted it off then sat down. It collapsed immediately, and he barely had time to let out a panicky "Wargh!" before he hit the floor.

THE MOON-Faced GHOUL-Thing

Ben helped him back to his feet. "I see why you're a Bad Luck Goblin."

"This? Ha! No, no, this is nothing, nothing at all," blurted Mr Nuttendudge. "I have a measurement scale, you see? Of unluckiness. I call it the Nuttendudge Scale."

"You named it after yourself?" said Ben.

Mr Nuttendudge blinked slowly. "Goodness. Yes. My word. So I did," he said. "I thought it sounded familiar."

He picked up another chair, looked at it for a moment then thought better of it. "Zero Nuttendudge is a day where nothing terrible happens. Nothing terrible at all. Theoretical, of course; I've yet to experience one," he said, wringing his oversized hands together. "Five Nuttendudge is the average. This? Why, this is barely a two."

There was a *crash* as part of his house fell over behind him. "Two and a half at most," he said, doing his best to smile.

Wesley scurried over and peered through the gap the collapsing wall had left. Acres of cloudy grey sky stretched overhead, and just twenty or thirty metres from the house stood the edge of a tall dark forest.

"Any sign of Scarrabus?" asked Ben.

Wesley shook his head. "Thankfully not."

Mr Nuttendudge's saucer-sized eyes somehow managed to grow even wider. "Scarrabus? Lord Scarrabus? Coming here? Why would he be coming here?"

"He was sort of chasing us," Ben explained. "We escaped his castle and stole his dragon."

THE MOON-Faced GHOUL-Thing

"We didn't steal his dragon, we freed his prisoner," Paradise corrected. She tickled the dragon under the chin. "Didn't we, Burnie? Yes we did! Yes we did!"

Mr Nuttendudge hobbled back and forth, shaking his oddly shaped head in dismay as he muttered to himself. "Lord Scarrabus. Coming here. Not good, not good. And them just children. Terrible. Terrible thing."

"It's not that bad," said Ben. "It's actually been kind of exciting so far. Don't you think?" He looked to the others and smiled. They didn't smile back.

"No," said Paradise.

"It's been horrible!" Wesley agreed.

"Come on!" said Ben. "Castle chases, weird monsters, dragons, dramatic escapes – it's been

pretty fun."

"Oh my no, oh my no," said Mr
Nuttendudge. "Lord Scarrabus is not fun,
not fun at all. Terrible. Terrible man. If he
finds you. . ." The goblin smacked himself on
the forehead, trying to drive an unwelcome
thought away. "No. He must not. He cannot."

"We'd really like to go home," said Wesley.
"Can you help us?"

Mr Nuttendudge stroked his cheekbrows
thoughtfully. "Perhaps. Yes. Perhaps. But
first . . ." He lowered himself carefully on to
another wooden chair and held his breath. The
chair stayed in one piece and the little goblin
relaxed. ". . . you must tell me everything."

chapter Nine

"Your guess is as good as mine," Paradise said.

She, Ben and Wesley had found broken bits of furniture among the wreckage and were perched in a semicircle around Mr Nuttendudge. Burnie had padded through from the kitchen and was curled up at Paradise's feet, snoring softly.

"One minute I was fast asleep in my bed, the next I'm being woken up by Wesley screaming."

"I wasn't screaming," Wesley protested. "I was . . . whistling."

"You were *whistling* 'Help me, help me, I don't want to die'?"

Wesley shifted on his stool. "Yes," he said. "I'm very talented."

Mr Nuttendudge nodded. He had nodded

THE MOON-FACED GHOUL-THING

at pretty much everything they had said, and
Ben was starting to wonder if his neck had
developed some sort of mechanical fault.

"Interesting. Yes.
Very revealing,"
the goblin mused.
"So, a servant
of Scarrabus
brought you
to his castle,
yes?"

"The Moon-
Faced Ghoul-
Thing," Ben
said.

Mr Nuttendudge frowned.

"The what?"

"The Moon-Faced Ghoul-Thing," Ben said again. "It's a sort of . . . thing."

"A sort of ghoul-thing," said Wesley.

"Yeah," Ben agreed. "It's a sort of ghoul-thing."

"With a moon-face," Wesley finished.

Mr Nuttendudge shook his head. "Never heard of it."

"It's got a big cloak and these kind of spider legs," explained Paradise.

"Oh, *that* servant of Scarrabus!" cried Mr Nuttendudge. He leaped to his feet dramatically, realised he looked a bit silly and so carefully sat down again. "Not Scarrabus's servant. His slave. Trapped. Forced to bring fresh victims into Goonderslarg."

"What is Goonderslarg exactly?" asked Ben.

THE MOON-Faced GHOUL-Thing

He and Paradise leaned forward on their bits of broken furniture as the goblin and Wesley explained in hushed whispers.

"It's a demon dimension," said Wes.

"One of the eight Monstrous Realms," continued Mr Nuttendudge. "Not the worst of them, perhaps, but still horrible. Horrible."

"Most of the scary things in our world — trolls, ogres, Shark-Headed Bear-Things — they come from one of the eight realms," said Wesley.

"Well, that's good," said Ben. "If they escaped then so can we."

"I still don't understand what we're even doing here," Paradise said. "We left out the sweets. We did everything we were supposed to."

"We did! We absolutely did," agreed Wesley. "Didn't we, Ben?"

Ben was suddenly taking a keen interest in a splodge of mud on his knee. He licked his thumb and tried to rub the smudge away, doing his best to pretend he hadn't heard.

"Ben?"

Ben looked up. "Hmm?"

"I said we left our tributes," Wesley said. "On the steps. For the Feast of Scarrabus. We left them out."

Ben cleared his throat. "Well, yeah. We. . . I mean. . . When you say 'left'. . ."

Paradise slowly got to her feet. With Ben sitting down, this made them almost the same height. She seemed to tower over him, though, as she fixed him with a glare so stern

THE MOON-Faced GHOUL-Thing

it could've shattered solid stone.

"What did you do?" she asked.

"What makes you think I did anything?" Ben asked, doing his best to sound innocent.

Wesley stood up. "Ben?" he said. "What did you do?"

Ben looked at both his friends in turn. He tried to smile, but the muscles in his face were having none of it and it came out all wonky.

"Itookallthesweetsback," he murmured all at once.

Paradise drew in a sharp breath. "What did you say?"

"You said yourself it was all make-believe, so I didn't think anything would happen," Ben explained. "And if it did it would just be a bonus."

"A *bonus*?" said Paradise. Wesley stood beside her, shaking his head, like he didn't want to believe what he was hearing.

"Yeah," said Ben. "We were bored. Nothing exciting had happened in months. I thought if the Scarrabus stuff was true, it might be – I dunno – fun."

"Fun?" Paradise growled. "You thought it might be *fun*? You idiot!"

THE MOON-Faced GHOUL-Thing

Wesley stepped between them. "Paradise, please. Let me handle this," he said calmly. He turned to Ben. "You *idiot*!" he yelped. "We weren't bored. *You* were bored. Not us. Not me. I love boring. Being bored is the most exciting part of my day!"

"I didn't think it would—"

"That's just it, Ben. You didn't *think*," said Wesley, clenching his fists and stamping his foot. "You never think, you just act. You act like everything's an adventure. Like danger is something to be laughed at!"

Sparks swirled around Wesley's clenched fists. Tiny flickering dots spun in his eyes, turning them into whirlpools of shimmering light. His voice took on a deep booming tone that seemed to shake the remaining walls of the house.

"But do you see us laughing, Ben?" he demanded, and flashes of power flitted across his teeth. "Do you see anyone here laughing about what you've done?"

Slowly, Ben stood up. "Easy, Wes," he said. He reached out to his friend, but a jolt of energy crackled up his arm, forcing him to jump back.

THE MOON-Faced GHOUL-Thing

"You've trapped us. You've doomed us to spend the rest of our lives stuck in this demon dimension *because you were bored*!"

"Calm down, Wesley," said Paradise gently. "He messed up, but he didn't know it was going to turn out like this."

Wesley spun to face her. Magical energy flickered across his face and fizzled through his hair. He unclenched his fists and a crackle of purple light trailed from his fingertips.

"Stop protecting him," said Wes in a voice like rumbling thunder. "Stop making excuses. Why do you always—"

WHAM!

A metal tea tray clanged against the back of Wesley's head. The magic glow sparked and flickered away. Wes's eyes crossed. He wobbled gently from side to side, said "Flibble," with quite a surprising amount of enthusiasm then fell over.

"Sorry about that," said Mr Nuttendudge, lowering the now badly dented tray. "Seemed like your friend was getting quite unfriendly."

Wesley lay face down on the floor in an X shape, his arms and legs spread out wide. Ben gave him a gentle nudge with the toe of his boot.

THE MOON-Faced GHOUL-Thing

"What was that about?" he wondered. "Since when was Wesley so. . ."

"Angry?"

"I was going to say 'magic'," said Ben. "He's normally useless at magic stuff."

The goblin gave his chin a thoughtful stroke. "The Feast of Scarrabus," he said. "It's the day of the year when the barriers between the Monstrous Realms are at their thinnest."

"Meaning?" asked Paradise.

"Meaning magic is flowing freely through all the dimensions. Even your own. Your friend has been soaking up dark sorcery and demoncraft for hours. He's dripping with evil magic now."

Wesley rolled on to his side, giggled something about kittens then began to snore.

"Are you sure?" Ben asked.

"Positive," said Mr Nuttendudge. "Certain. He'll probably swell up like a balloon and pop in a minute. Won't be pretty. No, sir. You might want to take a step back."

"What?" gasped Ben.

"Or find a waterproof hat."

"*What?*"

"There must be something we can do," Paradise said.

Mr Nuttendudge puffed out his cheeks, making him look even more toad-like. "We must get you home. Away from here. From the worst of the magic. We must find a way to open a portal out of Goonderslarg."

"Wait a minute! A portal, that's it!" Ben held up the gauntlet. "This opens portals!"

THE MOON-Faced GHOUL-Thing

Mr Nuttendudge hurried to his side. "It does? May I see?"

Ben hesitated. He knew the goblin was asking him to hand over the gauntlet, but it was his most precious possession in the world and he didn't like the idea of taking it off and passing it to someone he'd just met. Instead, he held his arm out so Mr Nuttendudge could get a closer look.

The goblin gave the gauntlet a sniff, then touched the tip of his thin purple tongue against the metal. He flicked his tongue around inside his mouth for a moment, analysing the taste, then his eyes went even wider with wonder.

"Wyrdanium," he gasped. "This metal, it's wyrdanium."

"What's wyrdanium?" Paradise asked.

"Only one of the most magical elements in existence," Mr Nuttendudge said. His fingers traced across the gauntlet's surface. "You say it makes portals? Where to?"

Ben looked at Paradise. They both shrugged. "Dunno," he admitted.

"I see. How do you activate it?"

THE MOON-Faced GHOUL-Thing

"There's a button on the back," said Ben. "Do you think it'll get us home?"

He made a move to press the button but Mr Nuttendudge caught him by the wrist.

"Not here!" the little goblin yelped. "At the circle."

"What circle?" asked Ben.

"The circle of the realms," said Mr Nuttendudge. "Through the forest, not far from here. One hour. Perhaps two."

He raised a spindly arm and pointed through the gap in the wall with his oversized hand. "The circle is the key. From there we can target it. Point you the right way. Open a portal there and home you will go."

"And you're sure about that?" asked Paradise.

"Certain, yes. Almost definitely. Probably."
He shrugged. "It's fifty-fifty."

Paradise nodded. "We've got to try."

Down on the floor, Burnie raised her head,
peered out through the hole in the wall and let
out a low growl.

Ben and Paradise followed her gaze. They
saw the forest with its twisted trees and
tangled branches. They saw the brooding grey
sky overhead. And within the forest's deep
shadows they saw something else. Something
round and white that seemed to be floating
through the darkness towards them.

Ben's stomach lurched, half with excitement
and half with fear.

It was back.

The Moon-Faced Ghoul-Thing was back.

chapter Ten

"Run, go, flee," urged Mr Nuttendudge, shooing the children towards a small door at the back of the house.

Ben and Paradise had Wesley's arms draped over their shoulders and were half carrying, half dragging him towards the door. He was stirring and groaning, but nowhere near awake enough to walk on his own.

Mr Nuttendudge hobbled ahead, unfastened
half a dozen locks and slide bolts then pulled
the door open, revealing an untidy garden
beyond. "Hurry, hurry."

Paradise looked back and saw the Moon-
Faced Ghoul-Thing float free of the forest.
Burnie was up on all four feet, her tail pointed
straight out behind her, her head lowered like
she was ready to charge.

"Come on, Burnie," she called, clapping a
hand against her thigh. "Here. Come here."

With a snarling yelp, the little dragon
launched herself through the gap in the wall
and bounded towards the approaching ghoul-
thing.

"Burnie, no!" Paradise cried. She moved to

THE MOON-Faced GHOUL-Thing

go after the little dragon but Ben stopped her.

"I'll go. You get Wesley out of here." He unhooked Wesley's arm from around his shoulder. Paradise immediately fell over beneath the sleeping wizard's weight. "Sorry," said Ben, helping them both up again. "Should have thought that through."

"I will get the dragon," said Mr Nuttendudge. "Find the well. Follow the tunnel within. The dragon and I will join you shortly."

Paradise glanced back again. Burnie was snapping and snarling at the Moon-Faced Ghoul-Thing but keeping a safe distance. The ghoul-thing floated on, ignoring her completely.

"Promise you'll get her," Paradise said.

"Promise. I promise. Get her I will," said
Mr Nuttendudge. "Now, go. The well. Hurry,
hurry."

Ben and Paradise stumbled out of the house
and along the garden path. The garden itself
was small and poorly kept, with tall grass
badly in need of cutting. Flowers had been
planted around the border,
but every one of them was
shrivelled and
brown.

THE MOON-Faced GHOUL-Thing

Mr Nuttendudge clearly didn't have much luck with gardening either.

On all sides stood the forest. It was the sort of forest it would be easy to get lost in, Ben thought, even with Paradise's finding ability.

Wesley's eyelids fluttered open. "Wh-what's happening?" he stammered.

"We're making a dramatic escape," said Paradise.

Wesley groaned. "Not another one. What are we escaping this time?"

"Moon-Faced Ghoul-Thing. Again," said Ben. He chewed his lip, then asked, "Are you OK, Wes?"

Wesley deliberately looked away and unhooked his arm from Ben's shoulder. "We're not running for the forest, are we?" he asked. "It looks terrifying."

"No, we're trying to find the well," said Paradise, before immediately tripping over and landing in a heap on the grass.

"Wow, you really *can* find anything," smirked Ben, pulling aside the tall grass to reveal a small stone well hidden within. They all peered down into the murky blackness.

The well was wide enough to climb down, but only if they went one at a time. Ben grabbed a stone from the ground, held it above

the well then let it fall.

Several seconds passed before they heard the faint *plink* of the stone hitting the water.

"It's a long way down," Paradise said.

Wesley stared at her in horror. "We're not climbing down there, are we?"

"There's a tunnel," Paradise said, her brow furrowed as she concentrated. "It leads away from the well and under the forest."

"The ghoul-thing won't be able to get us down there," Ben said. He slung a leg over the well and pressed his palms flat against the sides. "Come on, follow me."

Wesley shook his head. "Always rushing in," he muttered.

"Wesley's right," said Paradise. "We don't know what's down there."

"No, but we know what's up here," said Ben. "If the ghoul-thing is coming then so is Scarrabus."

Wesley looked back at Mr Nuttendudge's house, then peered past Ben into the well. "Oh, let's get it over with," he grumbled. He clambered into the well as Ben began to inch his way down.

THE MOON-Faced GHOUL-Thing

"I don't like this," Wesley said. "Have I mentioned that?"

"It'll be OK, Wes," said Ben, but the only answer from Wesley was a grunt as he began to clamber clumsily down the well.

When they were halfway down, they heard Paradise whisper, "I can't reach the walls. They're too wide."

"You mean your arms are too short," said Ben.

"Either way, I can't reach."

"Try," Ben urged. "Wedge your feet and back against the wall, and climb down that way."

From up above Ben heard Paradise mutter something under her breath. He heard the rustle of her robe as she got into position.

Then he heard her cry out in fright as her

feet slipped and she tumbled down the well towards him.

"Oof!"

"Careful!"

SPLASH!

They hit the icy-cold water in a tangle of arms and legs. Ben barely had time to gasp before he plunged beneath the surface.

Underwater, he could hear the muffled swishing of his friends, frantically fighting their way to the surface. He kicked out in the darkness, trying to swim upwards, but instead crashed into one of the well's stone walls.

He fumbled wildly, before a flailing foot caught him hard on the chin, spinning him round. The cold was making his body cramp. His lungs were crying out for air, but he had

THE MOON-Faced GHOUL-Thing

no idea in which direction he'd find any. Up, down, left, right, it was all the same down there in the cold darkness.

Something snagged him by the back of the tunic and yanked him sharply. With a *splosh* he broke the surface just as his mouth opened and he gulped in the damp well air.

"Are you OK?" Wesley asked. In the gloom, Ben could just make out that Wes had what looked like an inflated pig's bladder tied around each arm, keeping him afloat.

"I'm fine," Ben coughed. "Thanks, Wes. You saved my life."

Wesley looked surprised. "Did I? I mean, yes. So I did."

Ben gestured to the pig bladders. "What are those?"

"Arm floats," Wesley explained. "A little something I keep up my sleeve for just such an occasion. This robe gets *very* heavy when it's wet, so they help counteract the drag effect. Also, I can't swim."

Paradise gently cleared her throat. "Sorry. About the knocking us into the water thing.

THE MOON-Faced GHOUL-Thing

That was probably my fault."

Ben snorted. "Probably?"

"It's OK," said Wesley, cutting off the argument before it could start. "We all make mistakes. Don't we, Ben?"

Ben smiled at his friend, then nodded. "Can't argue with that." He looked around at the shadowy walls. "Now, where's this tunnel?"

Paradise concentrated for a moment, then gave a groan. "Oh great. Of course. It had to be."

"What's wrong?" asked Ben.

Paradise pointed downwards with her thumb. "It's down there," she said. "The tunnel is at the bottom of the well."

chapter Eleven

They swam in a line, Paradise leading the way, Wesley in the middle and Ben tagging along at the back. They had tied themselves together using a length of rope Wesley kept tucked up his sleeve. Although Paradise was small, her strong swimming strokes were practically pulling Ben and the non-swimming Wesley

along.

Paradise gave two sharp yanks on the rope, indicating that she had found the tunnel. Ben hoped it wasn't a long one — his lungs were already starting to ache and he couldn't hold his breath too much longer.

He swam down, feeling his way along the wall until he found a circular hole in the stone. Ben could tell from the position of the rope that Wesley had already followed Paradise into the tunnel. He was about to join them both when the rope suddenly went tight, slamming him against the wall.

Ben rolled clumsily into the passageway, pulled by the force of the rope. It dug into his waist, tightening around him like a snake, and he had to fight the urge to cry out in pain.

WHOOSH!

The water swept him
along, dragging him onwards, flipping
and twirling him out of control. He felt as if
he were being sucked down a plughole, and
every swirl and spin seemed to drain more air
from his lungs.

The rope tugged downwards. Ben bumped
and scraped along the rocky tunnel floor, then

THE MOON-Faced GHOUL-Thing

suddenly he was falling, plunging, down through the icy dark water.

Ben's head went light. Spots of colour swam before his eyes.

A tiny voice at the back of his brain was screaming at him to open his mouth and breathe, while another voice insisted he do the exact opposite.

This was it.

There was no escape.

He and his friends were going to die, and it was all Ben's fault.

His arms and legs went limp. His eyes began to close. His mouth relaxed and . . .

KERSPLOOOSH!

Paradise, Wesley and Ben were shot out of a hole in the ground on a towering spout of water. They coughed and spluttered and flapped their arms, then the gushing water stopped and they landed in three soggy heaps on the ground.

Wesley wheezed and retched and eventually spat out a very small, very startled frog. It shot him a disapproving look then hopped away into the forest.

"On s-second thoughts," Wes stammered. "Let's take our chances with the ghoul-thing."

It took a few seconds of struggling but the children eventually found the strength to get

THE MOON-Faced GHOUL-Thing

back to their feet, just as a little green man in sackcloth clothing came rocketing by them on another spout of water.

Mr Nuttendudge somersaulted through the air, bounced twice on the ground then eventually slammed face-first into a tree. A moment later, something fell from the branches and landed on his head. It was a wasps' nest.

Ben and the others watched as the Luck Goblin tore off into the forest, pursued by a swarm of angry wasps. They kept watching until his panicky screams had faded away completely.

"Cor," said Ben. "He *is* unlucky, isn't he?"

Paradise looked at the hole they had been fired through. The water had retreated once again. "Where's Burnie?" she said. "He said he'd get Burnie."

Her eyes darted across the dark forest around them, searching every shadow. "Burnie!" she called. "Burnie, where are you?"

Wesley clamped a hand across her mouth. "Sssh! You'll give our location away."

Paradise bit his finger, making him release his grip. "I don't care," she said. "We can't leave Burnie all alone."

"Ooh, that hurts," yelped Wesley. "That really hurts."

Ben put a hand on her shoulder. "Then find her," he said. "Use your ability to tell you

where she is."

"You nearly had my finger off!"

"I'm trying," Paradise snapped, ignoring Wesley. "Don't you think I'm trying? It's just . . . there's too much interference."

"That was practically cannibalism, that was!"

"What do you mean?" asked Ben, also ignoring Wesley.

Paradise looked at the trees. "I don't know. It's like . . . there are so many things around us. In the forest. Living things."

Wesley stopped hopping. "What sort of things?" he asked in a low whisper.

"S-something's coming," Paradise mumbled.

"Is it something nice?" asked Wesley hopefully.

Paradise's whole face twitched. "D-don't

149

know," she said. The word came out as a whimper. "Can't focus. This place . . . this whole forest is nothing but monsters. So many monsters!"

"Where's the closest one?" Ben pressed.

"I . . . I don't. . ." Paradise touched her head. She stumbled, and Ben barely managed to catch her before she hit the ground.

"Paradise, are you OK?" Ben asked, guiding her down on to the forest floor. "What's happening? What's wrong?"

Shaking, Paradise raised a hand and pointed past Ben's ear. "Th-there," she hissed. "The monster is there!"

Ben stood up and whirled round, just as a fast-moving shape exploded from the trees. The thing was small, but as it tumbled

THE MOON-Faced GHOUL-Thing

through the air towards him Ben got a fleeting glimpse of sharp claws and a long tail.

And then he saw nothing but the creature's red eyes and its long, pointed teeth.

And then he couldn't even see that.

chapter
Twelve

Ben staggered backwards, tugging at the
snarling ball of furious fur that had landed on
his face and immediately grabbed him by the
ears.

Giving a heave, he managed to pull the
creature off. It hissed and spat and slashed at
him with its claws. Its two large teeth snapped

THE MOON-Faced GHOUL-Thing

furiously and its long fluffy tail slapped against Ben's hand. Ben recognised the brute from Lunt Bingwood's monster guide.

"A Squirrel-Headed Squirrel-Thing!"

"So . . . what? It's got the head of a squirrel and the body of a squirrel?" asked Wesley.

"And the tail of a squirrel," added Ben.

Wesley glanced from Ben to the squirming thing in his grasp and back again. "That's just a squirrel, surely?"

Ben shook his head. "They're bigger and more ferocious."

His brow furrowed. He'd memorised most of Lunt Bingwood's monster guide off by heart, but the hissing and snapping of the Squirrel-Headed Squirrel-Thing was making it hard to concentrate.

"And . . . there's something else. . ."

"What?" whimpered Wesley. "Does it explode? Does it spit acid? What?"

"No, not that. . . It's. . ." Ben's eyes widened. "I've got it!" he cried. "They always travel in pairs!"

There was a rustling from high up in the trees. Another ball of fur came hurtling through the foliage and landed on the grass at Wesley's feet. It hissed at him, the hair on its back standing up on end. Before Wes could react, the squirrel-thing shot below his wet robe and scampered up his leg.

"Wuaaarghf!" Wesley shrieked, twisting and bucking around the clearing. "Hrumffgfeek!"

"Stay still," suggested Ben. "You'll make it angry."

THE MOON-FACED GHOUL-Thing

"It's already angry!" Wesley wailed, jigging and kicking and slapping desperately at his thighs. "Did you see its face? It's— *Ooh, don't you dare, don't you dare!* It's flipping furious!"

The first Squirrel-Headed Squirrel-Thing twisted free of Ben's grip and scampered up his arm. Its fluffy tail went around his neck and its claws dug into his scalp.

"Ow! Get off!" Ben barked.

He brought up the gauntlet to knock the squirrel-thing off, but it dodged and Ben slammed the metal glove against his forehead with a *clank*.

The squirrel-thing swung by its tail and flipped itself back up into Ben's face. It grabbed his ears with its clawed fingers and bit him on the end of the nose.

"Aaaargh!" Ben howled, just as Wesley came hopping and skipping past him, frantically punching at a scurrying lump beneath his robe.

Paradise climbed unsteadily back to her feet. She searched around until she found a heavy stick in the undergrowth. "Stay still," she told Ben, then she swung with the stick.

With a gleeful *chirp*, the squirrel-thing

scrabbled on to the top of Ben's head, just as the stick whacked him in the face.

"Yeeeow!"

"Sorry," said Paradise, swinging again. "I'll get it this time."

BONK! The stick clonked off the top of Ben's head just a split second after the squirrel-thing slid down on to his back.

"Will you *please* stop hitting me with that stick!"

"I'm only trying to help," said Paradise.

"Well you're—" The squirrel-thing dug its claws through Ben's tunic and into his back. "Yaaaaaargh! That stings. That really stings."

Wesley hurled himself past them and slammed his back against the ground, trying to squash the wriggling squirrel-thing. The moving bump scurried around to his front.

"Ooh! Eek! It's going for my belly button!" Wesley grimaced. "What if it finds a way in?"

Paradise swung with the stick, this time aiming at Wesley's middle. It hit him hard in the stomach, knocking the air out of him as the second Squirrel-Headed Squirrel-Thing squirmed out of the way.

THE MOON-Faced GHOUL-Thing

"Um, sorry," Paradise said. She looked at the stick. "I'm starting to think this is doing more harm than good."

"You reckon?" yelped Ben, spiralling past her as he tried to reach the squirrel-thing on his back.

He stopped spinning as a soft, haunting melody floated out from the forest. The clawing and scratching of the squirrel-things stopped too. Mr Nuttendudge stepped from the shadowy trees and into the clearing. He had a small wooden flute wedged up one nostril and was expertly playing a slow, lilting tune.

There was a *thump* from behind Ben as the squirrel-thing fell off him. Wesley jumped up and the creature that had been running amok

beneath his robe fell out. Both squirrel-things
snored gently in unison.

Mr Nuttendudge stopped playing. He pulled
the flute from his nose with a squelchy *schlop*,
then wiped it on his sleeve. "Goblin nose
flute," he said. "Works every time."

"You escaped the wasps,"
said Ben.

"Course I did,
course I did," said
the goblin. He
turned, and Ben
let out a "Yikes"
when he saw the
dozens of swollen
bumps on the back of
Mr Nuttendudge's head.

THE MOON-Faced GHOUL-Thing

"I mean, yes, obviously they stung me several hundred times on the head and face, but I escaped all the same."

"Where's Burnie?" Paradise asked. "Did you get her?"

Mr Nuttendudge's ears drooped. He shook his head gently. "I am sorry. She ran off. I could not stop her."

"But the ghoul-thing didn't get her?" Paradise asked.

"No," said the goblin. "No, of that I am sure." He beckoned them into the forest. "Now, hurry. The circle is this way. We must hurry. Hurry." He shot Wesley a worried look. "Before it's too late."

chapter Thirteen

Ben, Paradise and Wesley scampered along
behind Mr Nuttendudge, doing their best to
keep up.

Every so often the Luck Goblin would trip
on a vine, get snagged in a bush or walk
straight into a tree, but none of it slowed him
down for long.

THE MOON-Faced GHOUL-Thing

The children kept close together, their eyes scanning the woods for signs of danger. They didn't need Paradise's special ability to be able to spot the strange shapes and shadowy figures lurking in the trees on all sides. Mr Nuttendudge noticed them too, but he pressed on, paying them little heed.

"Are we almost there?" Wesley whispered.

"Yes, not far," said the goblin. "Not far. A few more minutes, that is all."

"How will it work?" Ben asked.

"Simple. You three will stand in the circle. I will take the gauntlet and let the circle's power guide its aim."

Ben stopped, making Wesley walk right into the back of him.

"Wait, what do you mean, you'll take the

gauntlet?"

Mr Nuttendudge didn't slow, so Ben hurried to catch up. "I must. It is necessary," said the goblin. "I will take the gauntlet and use its power to send you away. Home. Safe."

Ben looked down at the glove. Even in the darkness it seemed to shine. "But . . . it's my gauntlet."

This time it was Mr Nuttendudge who

stopped. He turned to Ben and shrugged. "Then keep it. Do as you wish." He leaned in closer and his wide eyes narrowed. "But it is your only hope. Without the circle, without my help, this . . . here. . ." He gestured at the forest around him. "This is home. Goonderslarg is where you will spend the remainder of your days."

"I don't fancy that," said Wesley.

Paradise looked at the glove, then up at Ben. "We don't have any choice, Ben," she said. "We can't stay here."

They all trudged on, leaving Ben behind. He flexed his fingers inside the glove. It was the most magical thing Uncle Tavish had ever seen. It was one of the very few connections he had to his parents.

And he was going to lose it. Forever.

Ben pushed through the trees and caught up with Mr Nuttendudge and the others at a point where the trees came to an abrupt stop. The tangle of grass and weeds became dry, barren sand. A wide desert stretched off into the distance, until it eventually met a load of angry-looking mountains coming the other way.

THE MOON-Faced GHOUL-Thing

About the length of a good stone's throw away stood nine tall rocks, positioned in a circle. Mr Nuttendudge set off towards them and the children followed quickly behind.

Overhead, an oblong-shaped sun beamed down at them, and by the time they reached the stones they were all slick with sweat.

"Here we are, here we are," breathed Mr Nuttendudge. He gestured for Wesley and Paradise to step into the stone circle, then held out a hand to Ben. "The gauntlet. Hurry. There isn't much time. Your wizard friend may explode at any moment."

"What?" spluttered Wesley. "No one told me this!"

Paradise pulled him into the space between the stones, explaining as they went. The air

around the circle gave a shimmer as they stepped through.

Ben peered down at his gauntlet and was surprised to find tears misting his eyes. He had got his friends into this, and if giving up his most prized possession was the only way to get them back out of it . . . well then, he had no choice.

"Give me the glove, boy," said Mr Nuttendudge. Ben blinked. The goblin was shifting nervously from foot to foot. His gaze darted hungrily from Ben's face to the gauntlet and back again. "Give it to me. Now."

Slowly, Ben took a step back. "I don't think I want to," he said. There was something about Mr Nuttendudge's expression that made him uneasy.

THE MOON-FACED GHOUL-THING

"Ben, look out!"

Paradise's warning came just in time. Ben spun, ducked and rolled, and barely avoided the swiping leg of the Moon-Faced Ghoul-Thing.

"Not yet, not yet!" wailed Mr Nuttendudge. "The glove, he hasn't given me the glove!"

Ben backed away from the ghoul-thing. "You set us up," he said, stabbing a finger towards Mr Nuttendudge. "You lured us here. Why?"

Wesley and Paradise raced over to join Ben, but as they reached the edge of the stone circle the air in front of them turned solid, forcing them back. Paradise hammered on the invisible barrier but they were trapped.

"Perhaps I can answer that," boomed a voice

THE MOON-Faced GHOUL-Thing

from within the Moon-Faced Ghoul-Thing's
cloak. An armour-clad leg emerged, then Lord
Scarrabus was unfolding himself from the
swirling portal within the cape.

The demon-lord drew himself up to his full
height, put his hands in the small of his back
and straightened his spine with a *crick*. "Oh,
that's better," he groaned. "That cape is such
an uncomfortable way to travel."

Ben looked back at Mr Nuttendudge.
The goblin was down on one knee, his
head lowered. "A thousand welcomes, Lord
Scarrabus," he said. "My worthless existence is
made all the more bearable by your presence."

"As you were, goblin," Scarrabus sighed.

"You betrayed us," snapped Ben.

Mr Nuttendudge blinked his wide eyes.

"Of course.
The servant of
Scarrabus and I
are old friends.
I arranged all this
while you made your
escape from my house.
You'd only just met
me. Whatever made you
think I'd be trustworthy?"
He opened and closed his
big hands like they were
flashing lights. "Stranger
danger, stranger danger!
Never trust a goblin you
don't know." He thought
about this for a moment.

THE MOON-Faced GHOUL-Thing

"Or one you do know. We're not to be trusted generally."

"Good work, Mr Nutty . . . thing."

"Nuttendudge."

"Whatever," said Scarrabus. "Bringing the children here was a stroke of genius."

"Why?" asked Ben.

Scarrabus smirked. "Because back at my castle I was merely going to imprison you," he said. "Here, I can use you."

"Use us?" asked Paradise.

"Use us f-for what?" Wesley stuttered.

"To tear open the dimensions. To rip asunder the very fabric of reality. To allow me access to your insignificant little world where everyone you have ever known will – at last – bear witness to a true Feast of Scarrabus."

"Yes! Yes!" sniggered Mr Nuttendudge.

Ben looked at the grinning Scarrabus and saw madness flash behind the demon-lord's eyes.

"It's going to be Hell on Earth!"

chapter Fourteen

For a few long moments, nobody spoke.
The silence was eventually broken by Lord
Scarrabus letting out a surprisingly high-
pitched giggle.

"Sorry, I can't do it. Your faces! You should
see your faces!"

"What?" said Ben. "What are you on about?"

"I'm not actually going to do those things, obviously," said Scarrabus.

"You're not?" said Paradise and Mr Nuttendudge at the same time.

"Why?" asked Ben, confused.

Inside the circle, Wesley threw up his hands in despair. "Well, don't make him think about it," he groaned. "He might change his mind again."

"Relax," laughed Scarrabus. "I was winding you up. I'm teasing. I'm not really going to tear open dimensions or that stuff. I wouldn't know where to start."

"I would," said Mr Nuttendudge under his breath. His wide eyes darted to Ben's gauntlet.

"But, but . . . you're evil," said Ben. "Aren't you?"

THE MOON-FACED GHOUL-THING

Scarrabus shrugged. "Well, I'm definitely mean. Aren't I?" He turned to the Moon-Faced Ghoul-Thing, who continued to stare eerily back. "Yeah, I'm definitely pretty mean, but I'm not evil as such. I was never going to hurt you really. This was all just a prank. It's what the feast is about. You leave a treat or you get tricked." Scarrabus laughed. "And I tricked you good!"

"A prank?" snapped Paradise. "You call this a prank?"

"I wasn't the one who jumped out of the window on the back of a dragon, love," Scarrabus reminded her. "If it had been up to me you'd have been home ages ago. Why do you think I had your clothes brought through? If I was going to keep you prisoner would I really have tried to make you more comfortable?"

He gestured towards the ghoul-thing. "Now, come on, let's get you home. You've had enough adventure for one night."

"I second that," said Wesley.

The Moon-Faced Ghoul-Thing didn't move.

"Come on, open the cape," Scarrabus commanded. "Send them back."

"Please," added Wesley.

The ghoul-thing's eyes darkened. Its cloak stayed firmly closed.

"Ah yes, how silly of me. Now I remember," sniggered Mr Nuttendudge. "This was the second part of my plan. My friend here is sick of being bossed around by the great and terrible Lord Scarrabus. We've been looking for

THE MOON-Faced GHOUL-Thing

a way to get rid of you for years."

With a flying grab, the goblin caught hold
of Ben's gauntlet and tugged. Ben yelped
in surprise as the glove slipped off and Mr
Nuttendudge scurried with it out of reach.

"And now we have one," Nuttendudge cried.

"Give that back," Ben barked, making a dive for the little goblin. Mr Nuttendudge's mouth moved as he muttered an incantation. The glove flashed purple and Ben was sent flailing backwards through the air. He slammed hard against one of the standing stones and landed in a crumpled pile on the sand.

By the time he got to his feet, all nine stones were lit up with the same purple glow. A bubble of indigo light was forming in the air above the circle. Paradise and Wesley backed away towards the centre.

Mr Nuttendudge squashed his oversized hand inside the gauntlet and his eyes lit up a violent shade of violet.

"That's enough, goblin," barked Scarrabus,

THE MOON-Faced GHOUL-Thing

stomping towards Mr Nuttendudge. The Luck Goblin muttered another enchantment. There was a flash and a *pop* and Scarrabus's golden armour fell to the ground as the demon-lord disappeared.

A moment later, a plump white rabbit hopped out from within the armour and blinked its glassy eyes in surprise.

"That was quite impressive," Wesley was forced to admit.

"There's more than one wizard around here," said Mr Nuttendudge.

"Why are you doing this?" Ben demanded.

The goblin's face twisted in rage. "Because I'm sick of it. Fed up. Taken all I can stand, and I can't stand no more. Five long decades living in Goonderslarg with only monsters

and bad luck for company. Five long decades
stuck in a Monstrous Realm while you and all
the other humans party it up in the dimension
next door. It's not fair!"

He placed his bare hand against the closest
stone. The energy bubble glowed brighter and
Wesley screamed in pain.

"Stop it!" Paradise cried. "You're hurting
him."

"What are you doing?" Ben demanded.

"I'm draining his magic. I'm draining
every last drop."

Ben made a run for the goblin again, but
the Moon-Faced Ghoul-Thing caught him
in its long spider arms.

"Thank you, old friend," said Mr
Nuttendudge. "Our time has come at last!"

THE MOON-FACED GHOUL-THING

Ben struggled against the creature's grip
but he didn't have the strength to break free.

He glanced sideways at Wesley, who was thrashing around on the ground.

"Why are you draining him? What are you going to do?"

"I'm going to crash you humans' party," sniggered the goblin. He raised the gauntlet above his head and lightning exploded from the fingertips. "And I'm going to bring some friends."

Wesley cried out again as the lightning from the gauntlet became a spray of purple fire that stretched all the way up into the clouds. Far overhead, Ben heard the rumble of thunder as the clouds began to bubble and boil.

"Stop," howled Paradise. "You're hurting him. Stop!"

Ben wrestled against the grip of the ghoul-

thing as
seven holes
tore open in
the sky above them.
Through the holes he saw
thousands of dark, twisting
shapes. They wriggled
and fought and squirmed.
It would surely be just
moments before they came
flooding through.

"The Monstrous Realms," Mr Nuttendudge
announced. "Ooh, aren't they horrible!"

"Why are you bringing those things here?" asked Ben.

"Oh, I'm not. No, sir." The goblin nodded in the direction of an eighth hole as it opened like a shutter in the sky. Through it, Ben could just make out the village of Lump. Home. It was so close and yet so impossibly far away.

"You can't," Ben pleaded. "You can't send them there. They'll destroy everything."

Mr Nuttendudge winked. "Yes," he said. "I know. That's the point. They'll swarm over there, clear it out, destroy each other, then we'll swoop in and rule what's left."

Ben tore his eyes away from the portal to home. He looked at the other seven, heaving and swarming with monsters and beasts and furious demons. He looked at Wesley, still

THE MOON-Faced GHOUL-Thing

writing on the ground as Mr Nuttendudge
used Ben's own gauntlet to bring about the
end of the world.

Tears welled up at the corners of Ben's eyes.

"I'm sorry," he shouted. "Wes, Paradise . . .
everyone. I'm sorry. This was my fault. I caused
this. You're right, I was an idiot."

*Somewhere, in an attic room in another world,
metal slid against stone.*

"I . . . I thought it was a game. I thought it
was all a bit of fun." He looked around, trying
to blink back the tears. "I never meant for any
of this to happen. I never meant for anyone to
get hurt. I put everyone in danger. It's all my
fault."

Above the sound of thunder there came
another noise. It was a low *whumming*, like

something spinning round and round at high speed. Mr Nuttendudge and Ben looked up, searching for the source of the sound.

Mr Nuttendudge squinted at a small black dot hurtling through the sky towards them. "What in Goonderslarg is that?" he said.

Ben's arm moved all on its own, with a strength that caught both him and the ghoul-thing by surprise. It broke the monster's grip and stretched up high, palm open, just as the hilt of a shimmering silver sword slapped against it.

Ben's fingers tightened around the handle. He recognised the monstrous carving on the hilt at once.

"My sword. This is my sword," Ben whispered. His hand and the sword moved as

one, swiping and swishing in a blur of speed.
The ghoul-thing squealed as its spider-like
legs fell to the ground.

Ben spun
round. The sword
flourished in a figure
of eight in front of
him, slicing the very air
itself to pieces.

"This is my sword,"
he said again, fixing Mr
Nuttendudge with a stern glare.
"And I am ready."

chapter Fifteen

Mr Nuttendudge muttered an incantation below his breath and a ball of green flame shot from the palm of his bare hand. Ben's sword immediately moved to block, and the fireball ricocheted off into the sky.

"More wyrdanium!" gasped the goblin. "Give it to me. I want it. I want."

THE MOON-Faced GHOUL-Thing

"Come and get it," Ben said.

Mr Nuttendudge's face twisted in anger. He launched two more fireballs, but Ben twirled and knocked them away. The goblin was still pointing the gauntlet to the sky, but the purple energy flowing from it spluttered, then stopped. Mr Nuttendudge looked at his hand and remembered he was supposed to be draining Wesley's magic.

The Luck Goblin reached for the stone. Ben leaped forwards, sword scything swiftly through the air.

Too late! Mr Nuttendudge's fingers found the stone. Wesley howled once more and an eruption of purple flame exploded from the gauntlet's fingertips.

It hit Ben full in the chest, sending him

skidding backwards across the sand. He
caught a glimpse of the creatures swarming
within the Monstrous Realms above, then Mr
Nuttendudge hit him with another bolt of

THE MOON-Faced GHOUL-Thing

concentrated magic.

Ben felt as if his body was turning inside out and his head was about to pop. He saw shadows creeping behind his eyes and realised he was going to pass out. A big part of him wanted to. Everything would stop hurting if he just gave up and fell unconscious.

But his friends were in danger, and giving up wasn't an option.

Ben gritted
his teeth.
He dug the
sword into
the ground
and leaned
on the handle.
Slowly, surely,
fighting
against
the pain,
Ben stood up.

"What? Impossible," spat Mr Nuttendudge.
"Stay down. I order you to stay down!"

"Not . . . going . . . to happen," Ben
grimaced. He took a faltering step towards
the goblin. Then another. Then another. The

THE MOON-Faced GHOUL-Thing

pain was immense, but nothing was going to stop him getting his glove back and saving his friends.

Or so he thought.

"Behind you!" Paradise yelped, but Ben turned too late. The Moon-Faced Ghoul-Thing hit him with a shoulder-barge, knocking him over and sending the sword sliding from his grip.

Keeping his hand on the magical barrier, Mr Nuttendudge hobbled closer. He sneered down at Ben. "Good try, boy," the goblin said. "Almost had me." He pointed the gauntlet towards Ben's head, palm open. "But now your time is up."

Mr Nuttendudge giggled. His eyes narrowed. His fingers spread wide.

And then, with a *ping*, his trousers fell down.

Instinctively, the goblin bent to pull them up, breaking his contact with the barrier. Ben swept with his foot, kicking Mr Nuttendudge's legs out from under him. The goblin flipped over in the air and landed on his long nose.

Ben scrabbled across the sand and grabbed for his sword, just as Mr Nuttendudge spat out a spell along with a mouthful of sand. The sword came up and deflected something Ben couldn't even see. There was a *pop* and the Moon-Faced Ghoul-Thing seemed to become a thousand different shapes all at the same time.

A second later, where the ghoul-thing had been, there was now a large frog in a tiny robe. It hung in the air for a moment looking really

THE MOON-Faced GHOUL-Thing

quite surprised, and then gravity
took hold and it landed with
a *splot* on the sand.

Mr Nuttendudge
kicked backwards
along the ground.
Before Ben could reach him, he slapped a hand
against another of the standing stones and
grinned triumphantly.

Nothing happened. He adjusted his
fingers, splaying them flat against the stone.
The goblin stared at it in disbelief. "It's not
working. Why isn't it working?"

"Like you said," called Paradise. "There's
more than one wizard around here."

Ben turned to see Wesley floating towards
them, a metre or so above the ground. Wes

giggled as he skimmed along above the sand, wobbling unsteadily. Paradise ran behind him, her little legs struggling to keep up.

"Magic," Wesley said. "Look at me . . . I'm doing magic."

"Looking good, Wes," Ben told him.

Mr Nuttendudge scowled. "You'll never get the gauntlet. It's mine now. All mine!"

He held up his hand. The gauntlet was no longer there. "Oh, trollfarts," he cursed.

"It fell off when you were talking," said Ben, stooping to pick up the glove.

Paradise smirked. "How unlucky."

Ben looked up at the holes in the sky above them. Shapes were now swarming through, making their way from the other Monstrous Realms into this one. Soon they'd find a way

THE MOON-Faced GHOUL-Thing

back to the human world. There was no time to lose.

"How do we stop it?" Ben demanded.

"I'll never tell you!" Mr Nuttendudge cried. Ben pointed the sword at his throat. "OK, OK, I'll talk! No need to get nasty."

The goblin took a deep breath. "There's just one spell you can use to stop it. One incantation you need to say. Ready? What you need to say is—"

An enormous black rock fell from the sky, squishing Mr Nuttendudge flat. Ben, Paradise and Wesley leaped back, just as five more of the boulders slammed into the ground around them.

One by one the stones unfolded, becoming
large rock creatures before the children's eyes.

"That's not good," Ben gulped.

"What do we do?" asked Paradise.

Ben puffed out his cheeks. "I'm at a bit of a
loss," he admitted. "Run away?"

"No."

Ben and Paradise turned in disbelief to
Wesley. "Did you just vote against running
away?" Paradise asked.

Energy crackled from Wes's fingertips. "I can
feel it," he said in a whisper. "All the magic in
all the worlds. I can feel it."

"It's too much," said Ben, backing away from
the rock creatures. "It could make you blow
up."

Wesley gazed up at the holes in the sky.

THE MOON-Faced GHOUL-Thing

Other shapes were already tumbling through into Goonderslarg. "No. I can control it. I can close the holes," he said. "I can send them all back. I just need a minute."

"Not sure we have a minute," said Paradise. The rock-headed rock-things were closing in a circle. Any second now, they'd be upon them.

"Keep them busy," said Wesley, and with a sweep of his arm he drifted straight up into the sky.

Ben and Paradise watched him go. "'Keep them busy,' he says," Ben sighed. He tightened his grip on the sword and eyed up the monsters around him. They were each over three metres high, with fists like solid slabs.

"I'll take the one on the left," Ben said, standing back to back with Paradise. "You take the other five."

"Sounds fair," Paradise said.

Ben smiled, but it didn't
last long. "I'm sorry," he said.

THE MOON-FACED GHOUL-Thing

"This is all my fault."

"Oh, stop going on about it," Paradise said. "You made a mistake. We forgive you, OK?"

The closest rock creature raised its arms and stepped closer. Ben swung with his sword at its leg. The blade struck the stone with a *bdoing* and Ben felt his whole body vibrate.

"Ow-w-w-w-w-w!"

Paradise dragged him back. They stumbled and fell together on to the sand.

A rock-thing loomed above them and the children braced themselves for the end.

A tiny ball of flame burst against the creature's face. It shook its head, irritated, just as three more little fireballs exploded on the side of its neck.

Paradise and Ben scrambled to their feet. Something reddish-pink and bull-sized bounded across the sand, spraying pellets of fire from its throat. The rock-things hissed and swatted at the flames as Paradise squealed in delight.

"Burnie!"

There was a sonic boom from overhead. The clouds swept aside as bolts of electric-blue power snaked from Wesley's fingertips. With a sharp jerk, the rock-things were yanked

THE MOON-Faced GHOUL-Thing

sharply upwards like fish on a hook. They tumbled through the sky, then flipped and flopped back through the hole they'd come through.

All around Ben and Paradise, the other creatures were also being dragged back to their Monstrous Realms. Ben punched the air in delight. "He did it! Wesley did it!"

As the last of the creatures was pulled back into the portals, the holes began to close. At the very same time, Wesley's lightning vanished. He flapped his arms. He let out a very unwizard-like sob.

"I've run out of magic," he yelped.

And then, with all that out of the way, he began to fall.

chapter Sixteen

"Catch him!" Paradise shouted.

Ben looked from her to Wesley and back again. "What, me?"

"Anyone!"

Wesley was falling too fast. He twirled around in a tangle of robes, the wind spinning him as he plunged towards the ground. "Feel free to rescue me any time!" he shouted.

THE MOON-Faced GHOUL-Thing

"Hey!" Paradise yelped, as Burnie bumped into her. Paradise fell on to the dragon's back just in time for Burnie to scoop Ben up with her long neck.

With a groan of effort, the little dragon hurled herself into the air and beat her stubby wings. Ben and Paradise grabbed on tightly as Burnie lurched sideways and bounced on the sand.

"You can do it, Burnie!" Paradise cheered.

"I doubt she can," said Ben. He caught Paradise's look. "I mean . . . you can do it, Burnie!"

With a hiss of effort the little dragon began to climb. She banked upwards until she was above Wesley, then swooped down. Her claws snatched at him, snagging his robe and

stopping his fall
with a sudden jerk.

Wesley stopped
screaming for a few brief moments, then
started again when Burnie began to fly higher
and higher towards the sky.

"No, go down!" he cried. "The ground's that
way!"

"She's not aiming for the ground," Ben

realised. He pointed ahead to one of the holes in the sky. It was the last hole to have opened. It was the last hole to start closing. It was the hole that led home.

"Go, Burnie, go!" Paradise urged. The dragon was struggling with the weight of all three children. She flapped and flapped, but the hole was closing over too fast.

"We're not going to make it," Wesley wailed. "We're too heavy."

Ben looked down at the gauntlet and the sword. He looked at the hole in the sky. He had been the one to get his friends into this and there was no way he was leaving them trapped here. No matter what the cost.

With a deep breath, Ben tossed his gauntlet and sword away.

"No!" Paradise yelped. She grabbed for them but they were already tumbling towards the ground far, far below. "Your gauntlet. Your sword. They're important."

Ben shrugged. "There are some things even more important," he said, then he leaned down low and gave the dragon an encouraging pat. "Now go, Burnie. Get us out of here!"

With a screech, Burnie beat at the air. The hole was just ahead of them now, but closing fast. They rocketed towards it, the wind whipping at them and stinging their eyes.

THE MOON-Faced GHOUL-Thing

"We're not going to make it!" said Paradise.

"Yes," said Ben as they streaked towards the shimmering purple glow. "We are!"

There was a sound like rushing water, a flash of white, a scream of Wesley and then . . . there was nothing at all.

Ben opened his eyes in time to see a large dragony tongue lick his face. He spluttered and sat up, pushing Burnie away. "Ew, get off."

He was lying in a grassy field, covered in twigs and clumps of mud. Paradise and Wesley propped themselves up beside him. They looked one another over. "Anyone broken anything?" Wesley asked.

"Nope," said Ben.

"I'm OK," said Paradise. "And nobody

landed on me this time, which was a nice bonus."

Ben looked up at the blue sky overhead. It was dotted with fluffy white clouds. There wasn't a portal to a demon dimension in sight. "So," he said, "are we—"

"Home!" said Paradise, getting to her feet. "We're back home. We're just a few miles from Lump."

Wesley leaned down and kissed the ground. "Oh, the World, how I've missed you."

He and Ben stood, enjoying the feeling of

the sun on their backs. Burnie circled them, her tail wagging excitedly.

"You know who I feel a bit sorry for?" asked Paradise.

"Me?" said Wesley. "I had a terrible time."

"Scarrabus. I wonder what's going to happen to him."

Wesley fished up his sleeve. After a moment, he pulled out a large white rabbit. "Ask him yourself," he said, passing her the demon-lord-turned-bunny.

"I think I prefer him like this," Paradise said, tickling the rabbit under the chin. She tucked Scarrabus under one arm. "Let's go. Home's this way."

She skipped off in the direction of the village. Wesley hurried along behind her. They both stopped when they saw Ben looking at his bare hand.

"Oh, Ben. I'm sorry about your gauntlet," Paradise said.

"And the sword," said Wesley. "You'd just got it too."

Ben waggled his fingers. "It's OK," he said.

The others gathered around him. "They were important. They were clues to your family," Paradise said.

Ben smiled. "Guys, it's fine. Besides," he looked at them both in turn, "I've already got a family."

The three friends didn't speak for a few long moments, until Paradise eventually broke the silence.

"Wow, that nearly made

THE MOON-Faced GHOUL-Thing

me throw up in my mouth," she said.

"Yes, that was truly corny," Wes smirked.

Ben laughed. "Ah, shut up," he said. "Let's go home."

And, with Scarrabus the rabbit under one arm, and Burnie the dragon trotting alongside them, they all did just that.

Together.